Reasons of the Heart

By the same author

Scandal's Daughter

Reasons of the Heart

JOANNA ERLE

ROBERT HALE · LONDON

© Joanna Erle 2001
First published in Great Britain 2001

ISBN 0 7090 6928 6

Robert Hale Limited
Clerkenwell House
Clerkenwell Green
London EC1R 0HT

2 4 6 8 10 9 7 5 3 1

Typeset by
Derek Doyle & Associates, Liverpool.
Printed in Great Britain by
St Edmundsbury Press, Bury St Edmunds, Suffolk.
Bound by Woolnough Bookbinding Limited

Author's Note

The mysterious hole – thought to have been made by a bullet – appeared in the window of the Regent's carriage on a public occasion three years later than the event for which I have borrowed it.

J.E.

The heart has its reasons which reason does not know.

Pascal

Reason has moons, but moons not hers,
Lie mirrored in her sea,
Confounding her astronomers,
But, O! delighting me.

Ralph Hodgson

CHAPTER ONE

'*B*olt the door!'

The shrill cry dragged Elaine from a depth that was more a stupor of exhaustion than sleep. Heart pounding, she stumbled up from the low cot-bed on which she had been resting.

'What is it, Aunt Marney? What is it?'

A half-burned tallow candle gave meagre light in the bleak room but enough to show her the door standing blackly ajar on the still and silent house; enough to reveal, too, in the shadows cast by the tattered curtains of the ancient four-poster bed, an old woman sitting upright, a quivering finger pointing.

'Bolt the door! Don't let him in!' she repeated, her voice as strong and harsh as ever it had been.

Carefully, Elaine eased the shrunken figure that in the past eight days and nights had not moved a limb without help, back against the pillows. 'There's no one there, Aunt,' she said. 'It's past midnight. You've been dreaming.' Dreaming, as so often before, of Phillip Walden, the sea-captain who had jilted her more than forty years ago.

Looking up at Elaine from under drooping, red-veined lids, the woman's eyes splintered bright malice. 'He's too late, gel! Too late. Tell him that.' She muttered more, her voice beginning to weaken, but gathering strength again to rasp as Elaine bent nearer to hear her, 'Don't crowd me!' Her scowl deepening, her head fretted weakly to and fro on the pillow emphasizing rejection. Then, almost as strongly as before, she declared, 'There's no bait in it for the men, you'll find. None! Be damned to 'em!' Her sigh was an expression of rare satisfaction. It lengthened, changed to a harsher sound – and was her last use of breath in this world.

Her mind clogged with tiredness, it took several minutes for Elaine to accept that Sarah Marney was dead. Acceptance brought no feeling. With bitter wonder she remembered that there had been a time when she had prayed for Sarah's death – prayed with a child's passion for the only release from a hated life that she could see. She shrugged the memory away with dreary indifference: that had been before hunger and hardship had drained all passion out of her. After eight years under Sarah Marney's despotic rule it would be wonderful, indeed, if she had any capacity for feeling left in her.

Looking down at the earthly shell of Sarah's unkind spirit she saw only an old, old woman with fallen jaw and the pinkness of her scalp showing through thin, cropped white hair . . . a little corpse so withered and frail it scarcely mounded the bed-clothes. Tyranny should surely look more impressive. . . .

The funeral was over. The only mourners had been Elaine and John Woolford, the lawyer who had come each quarter-day to put into Sarah's hand the small sum of money on which she and Elaine subsisted.

Now, his hand at Elaine's elbow, John Woolford was hurrying her through the rainy dark out of the churchyard to where his carriage waited in the lane.

'We shall both feel more comfortable after a little supper in one of The Griffin's private rooms where we are to meet your cousin, Mr Marney,' he told her as he helped her into the waiting chaise.

The journey was quick, and before long Elaine found herself in a room bright with lamplight and a generous fire, comforts she had almost forgotten existed. She gave them little notice, all her thoughts now centred on the arrival of her unknown cousin. Since Mr Woolford's discovery that she had, after all, one relation left in the world, she had been longing for this meeting, certain he would deserve all the golden opinions she was waiting to bestow on him. Coming from Tunbridge Wells, he was due to arrive at any moment and she prayed he would not be late.

A bustle in the passage outside the room told her he was here . . . was entering the room. With a surge of pleasure, she saw a young man just above medium height, with a well set-up figure, black curling hair and eyes of a vivid blue made more noticeable by thick, spiky black lashes. His skin was a ruddy brown, his looks attractively masculine. The confidence with which he entered the room suggested he knew what it was to please.

Mr Woolford, moving forward to greet the newcomer, had given Elaine time to make her study. Now the two men turned towards her.

In one swift sweep, her cousin's blue gaze passed over her from head to foot and into it came the unmistakable and merciless reflection of what he saw. Her own gaze dropped from his as though struck away and there, clenched awkwardly before her, were her hands, a servant's hands, red, scarred and ugly with everyday drudgery and protruding from the frayed cuffs of a gown that had suffered every kind of hard usage. With a force she had never known before, she was made aware that the made-over gown hung gracelessly about the starved figure of a drab and charmless woman. She stood exposed by that gaze for no longer than a moment, but it was long enough to set an impassable gulf between them and destroy forever the fragile hopes and dreams she had held of finding a friend.

'A glass of Madeira, Miss Marney. It will help to drive out the damp and cold.' Mr Woolford was between them now, having missed nothing of the nuances of the cousins' meeting. Smiling encouragingly at Elaine, he guided her to a chair and when she was seated, put a glass in her hand. He waited long enough to see her begin to sip the drink, then turned to engage her cousin in a polite discussion of the chances of a peace treaty being signed with the Americans before Christmas now that that wasteful and abortive war was over.

Elaine continued to sip at her wine hardly aware that she did so. Her small stock of energy had drained from her, but by the time her glass was empty the bitterness of her disappointment had dulled. By then, too, the last of a number of hot dishes had been brought to the sideboard and a waiter was inviting them to take their seats at the table.

Despite having such a meal set before her as she had not seen for a long time, Elaine found she had no appetite for it. Suddenly, she was drowning in tiredness and unused to making conversation, the effort seemed beyond her. She knew that Mr Woolford looked at her with anxious attention from time to time, knew, too, that in his kindly, courteous way, he covered her silence as much as lay in his power. Once or twice Oliver directed a remark towards her, raising his voice and spacing his words carefully as though addressing someone whose wits were lacking. Her replies were short and, she thought uncaring, no better than he expected.

When only dessert and decanters stood on the table and the waiter had withdrawn, Mr Woolford glanced from one to the other of his guests and said, 'Now we are comfortable, it is time, I think, to introduce the matter of Miss Sarah Marney's will.' Taking a folded document from an inner pocket he laid it on the table before him.

The word 'will' speared through Elaine's apathy, briefly waking a long-dormant sense of the ludicrous. That Sarah should have thought what she had to leave worth the dignity of a will to dispose of could not be thought other than risible. Belatedly, she realized that Sarah's income – minute though it was – must have had a source.

That source was soon revealed as a sum of £500 invested in a Government Fund yielding three per cent. And that Sarah had left to her great-nephew, Oliver Marney.

It was too much a part of Sarah's unending delight in working mischief to occasion Elaine pain, but Mr Woolford had not finished reading, and her own name called her attention back to him as he read:

. . . I devise and bequeath all else of my property both real and personal whatsoever and wheresoever situate unto my great-niece Elaine Luce Marney until marriage so that she may be provided for in her single state. Subject thereto I give devise and bequeath all my real and personal property to my great-nephew Oliver Marney absolutely.

Familiar as she was with the 'all else' of Sarah's property, wry laughter rose in Elaine. And then, adding to her bitter amusement, she looked up to find Oliver's glittering, speculative gaze fixed on her. He turned from her to Mr Woolford to ask in a tone divided between curiosity and a sneer, 'My late mother's opinion was, I remember, that my great-aunt owned nothing of worth beyond the sum that provided her income – so what remains?'

The lawyer looked down at the parchment he held, his lean, rather austere face carefully expressionless as he chose his next words. Before he could speak however, Elaine, her mind suddenly awake, found a voice, a voice sharp with derision.

'There is a dwelling, sir, reached by way of an alley long known as Sluts' Hole. A well-ventilated place where wind and rain enter as freely as ever did my great-aunt and I, and where one is rarely without the company of its other tenants. Tenants who do not, I regret to say, pay rent, being all of the furred or feathered kind. As for furniture – there is sufficient, I think, to start a smallish bonfire, that being the most useful purpose to which it is now likely to be put.'

The sudden quickening into acid-tongued fluency of the creature he had supposed, at best, feeble-minded, shook Oliver's complacency for a moment. Staring at Elaine, he took in what he had not noticed before – that her eyes were long and green and the gleam in them as she stared back at him revealed an all too keen intelligence. God in heaven! he thought, she looks like nothing so much as a starving alley cat! A cat with claws. . . . Well, if the house she described was all she inherited, cousin or not, she need not look to him for help. He turned to Mr Woolford to make the point clear.

'If that is all Miss Elaine inherits, how is she to support herself? It is beyond my power to assist her.'

Elaine's laughter rose nearer the surface. Sarah would have been proud of Oliver, so truly her natural heir. And this was the man she, Elaine, had longed to meet!

John Woolford had taken Oliver Marney's measure very quickly. His long-fingered hands folded the will back into its creases with deliberate care while the silence lengthened, isolating Oliver's last words. Only when the document had been returned to the inner pocket of his dark, well-cut coat did he look up. His smiling gaze rested on Elaine. It was clear to him that, as yet, she had no idea of what her inheritance gave her. Nor – a sobering thought – of what it robbed her. Looking at the gaunt woman before him, he could not help remembering the lively attractive child she had been when she was first sent into Sarah Marney's care.

Care! How different the truth had been. A year from her eightieth birthday, Sarah Marney – increasingly nursing her obsessions and increasingly malicious – had been suffering the ills of age

14

made worse by the harsh conditions in which she lived. Her orphaned great-niece had come conveniently to hand at the time of Sarah's greatest need. Children were the property of their relatives. Lacking anyone with greater claim, there had been no way Elaine could be rescued from becoming Sarah's drudge. Through the eight following years, his visits to the old woman had shown him, quarter by quarter, the sparkling child's transformation into a worn-down creature whose life was bounded by the demands of simply supplying everyday needs.

With a malicious satisfaction quite foreign to him, John Woolford explained what the 'all else' of Sarah Marney's will meant.

Nodding at Oliver, he said, 'You, sir, saw your great-aunt only once when you were a boy of twelve, so you told me, so you may not know that the lady had certain eccentricities stemming from a grievous disappointment. At the time that it occurred, she was living on the income from the five hundred pounds left to her by her father – a sum that provided more comfort then than in more recent years. At the time of which I speak, Miss Marney was approaching her fortieth year and was happily engaged to be married to a half-pay sea-captain.'

Alive to Oliver Marney's growing impatience, he was in no mood to give him quick relief and paused to sip appreciatively at his brandy, its sinfully fine quality suggesting an unlawful and untaxed entry into the country. Putting down the glass, he said then, 'In those days, my father had charge of Miss Marney's affairs. Later, when handing them over to me, he told me that the prospect of marriage had been a great thing to her and that the shock of being jilted in favour of a widow with a greater income – and that a little more than a week before the wedding – quite overwhelmed her.'

It was an old story to Elaine, Sarah's bitterness never having abated one jot through the years. Why, she wondered, was Mr

Woolford troubling to relate it to Oliver? He, she was sure, would have no interest in anyone's disappointments but his own. There was however, a curious little smile on the lawyer's lips that held her own attention steady.

'By an irony of fate, a month after that unhappy event, Miss Marney found herself heiress to a small fortune. Having no heirs of his own, a man for whom her father had once done great service, left what he had made by successful enterprise in America to the woman he thought to be his benefactor's only child. In fact, Miss Marney had two young brothers who, in time, each fathered a son from whom you are separately descended. Having become an heiress, Miss Marney, perhaps not unreasonably, thought she might now be sought in marriage solely for what she had. It was a point on which her mind became more and more deeply disturbed. Not only did she keep her newly acquired fortune secret from her family, but she refused to make use of it herself. Though she accepted my father's advice as to the money's safe and rewarding investment, she refused all thought of using any part of the income from it. The knowledge of her fortune's safety and continuing increase was all the pleasure and comfort Miss Marney ever derived from it.'

The silence that followed stretched through long moments before words burst from Oliver as though impossible to contain. 'My God! Forty-seven years or more have gone by since then! The old witch must have been as mad as my mother thought her. What, in the name of all that's holy, does the sum amount to now?'

His lips shaping a faint distaste, Woolford turned from the man to bend a solicitous look on Elaine. 'Suffice it to say, Miss Elaine will enjoy an income that will ensure her future ease and independence.'

Silence again. Elaine sat white and still, unable to bring herself to believe what the lawyer had said. Memories crowded in on her

16

of the bitter cold of the winters she had endured in the years since her parents had been swept out of her life by a cholera epidemic . . . memories of ice thick on those panes of glass that remained entire in the hovel she had been despatched to share with Sarah . . . and Sarah herself, a shrivelled malevolence seemingly forever crouched over the one inadequate fire. Memories of endless hunger . . . of hours spent in darkness for want of candles . . . of her late childhood and early girlhood wasted in an endless expenditure of effort to meet all the miserable shifts and contrivances that abject poverty required to ensure she and Sarah survived. *And all unnecessary!*

Grey desolation swept her. Her heart thudded uncomfortably in her breast and a desperate need for more air jerked her to her feet. Turning to the door, she rushed from the room.

CHAPTER TWO

Cato Raffen stepped into the welcoming warmth of The Griffin's broad entrance passage and with relief closed the door on the cold, evil-smelling fog that was beginning to form outside. Sweeping off his moisture-beaded hat, he was half out of his heavy riding-coat when a woman rushed through a nearby doorway, took one blind, swimming step towards him and crumpled to the ground.

Dropping coat and hat, Cato crossed the small distance to the slight, shabby figure and lifted it into his arms. As he did so, two men came through the doorway from which the woman had run. The large young man leading made no move to take Cato's burden from him, but stood staring down at her with a look of repugnance on his coarsely good-looking face. The other, older man, pushing past, wore an expression of deep concern.

Though they had met for the first time six days ago, recognition was mutual and instant. 'In here. Mr Raffen, if you would be so good.' John Woolford stood aside to allow him to pass.

The inn was not one that catered for the hurly-burly of the public coaches, but drew its chief business from the more discerning carriage trade passing through Highgate. The room beyond the doorway was comfortably furnished for private use and an ancient brocaded sofa offered ample accommodation for the woman's slender form. When he had laid her on it, Cato gazed down at her with wry sympathy.

The pathetic scrap had weighed nothing; indeed, had felt like a mere bundle of skin and bones beneath her shabby garments. A half-starved drudge from an impecunious house, he guessed. One of those unfortunate creatures who, in the twenty-five or six years she had lived in an uncaring world, had received little but harsh treatment from it. Endowed with scant visible charm, her hair hung lank and lifeless where it had escaped its pins and the bones of her face thrust harshly into notice under an almost translucent covering of deathly pale flesh. If she had any claim to womanly attraction, it lay in the finely arched brows and long, silken lashes crescented on her cheeks. Yet there *was* something more, he mused . . . a delicacy, a vulnerability, even a sweetness. . . .

He moved aside as Woolford came to the sofa with a glass of brandy and glanced about him. The curiosity that was second nature to him was awake now. The two men and the woman made an oddly assorted trio to have dined together, as the dishes standing on the central table showed.

What, he wondered, had brought together Woolford, the gentlemanly lawyer, the flashily attired young buck and the careworn woman? More interestingly, what had pushed that same woman into headlong flight? For flight it surely had been. But for Woolford's obvious concern for her, his curiosity might have taken on the darker tone of suspicion. As it was, it was none of his business, he told himself, but could not resist saying, 'The young woman looks in a fragile state of health.'

'She has endured a long period of strain,' the lawyer returned unexpansively. He looked up from where he was kneeling to administer the brandy. 'Accept my thanks for your help, Mr Raffen. We must not trespass further on your kindness, however. You and I will meet as arranged in a month's time when I trust I shall have more information regarding the matter we discussed.'

It was dismissal. Whatever small mystery there was, he was not to be allowed to share in it. Mildly amused at his own sense of disappointment, Cato bowed and walked from the room.

It was to be a winter to remember.

Slowly, throughout the week before Christmas, the fog thickened and spread to lie like a curse on the land for three whole weeks, halting traffic, delaying the mails and causing many and bizarre accidents. The New Year of 1814 was four days old before it cleared.

Two days later, Cato rode under a leaden sky through a countryside now thickly rimed with frost towards his second appointment with John Woolford. A prisoner of the weather, he had had ample time to reflect on the folly of returning to England from warmer climes in early December. It was providential, he thought, that John Woolford lived on the outskirts of Highgate and had offered him the convenience of meeting at his home instead of at his Gray's Inn rooms as before. It meant a shorter journey through the bitter cold.

The lawyer's house was soon reached. It came into view at the end of a well-kept gravelled drive, its size and grace mildly surprising him. Unmistakably, it had been built to an asymmetrical Italianate design of John Nash's at his picturesque best, having a round tower, broad eaves and an elegant arcade along the front. The maturity of the small park in which it was set suggested that once an older house had stood in its place, a house that perhaps had fallen into decay and been demolished.

Cato's arrival was anticipated. A groom appeared to take charge of his horse as soon as he dismounted and before his hand could touch the knocker, the door was opened by a plainly dressed manservant. Passing into a marble-tiled hall, pleasantly warmed and scented by burning applewood in an open fireplace, he was shown into a long bookroom lit by tall windows. With a murmured, 'Mr Woolford will be with you in one moment, sir,' the servant left him.

It was a handsome room, handsomely furnished. Divided by an archway hung with damask curtains of a rich dark green looped back with heavily tasselled ropes of dull gold silk, the half of the room he had entered was dominated by an impressive desk backed by bookcases holding weighty-looking leather-bound tomes such as might be thought worthy of codifying the law.

Having surveyed his immediate surroundings, Cato halted, his thoughts turning to the business that had brought him here. In the next moment however, the unsleeping sixth sense that had more than once saved his life, warned him that he was not alone in the room.

Glancing through the archway, he saw a woman standing on the platform of a short flight of library-steps. She was facing him, a large volume clasped to her chest, her thin body rigid, her expression blank enough to give the impression she had been turned to stone. Amusement lit his eyes. Strolling through the archway to the foot of the steps, he thought it fortunate it was not his most usual effect on those of the feminine gender.

Looking up at the woman, he held out a hand, saying with a smile, 'I'm sorry if my arrival startled you. Allow me to relieve you of that heavy volume.'

Even as he spoke, Cato recognized her: this was the same young woman he had picked up from the flagstoned passage of The Griffin three weeks ago. There was a slight improvement in her appearance. but much remained of the look of desperate frailty that had first woken his compassion. What was new to him was the colour of her eyes: against the pallor of her face their greenness was striking. There was some betterment in her apparel, but his observant gaze saw at once that her gown had been made-over from one belonging to someone of quite different height and shape. So . . . possibly a poor relation, but more probably – as he had thought before – a servant.

There had been no reaction to his words and he began to wonder if she was simple-minded, perhaps employed by Woolford out of charity. Compassion stirred in him again and he prompted gently, 'Your descent from Olympus will be eased, you know, if you give me the book.'

As though stung, she thrust it at him, walked down the steps and held out her hands for its return. Her lips moved soundlessly and he supposed she thanked him in the moment before she scurried towards the door. Anticipating her eagerness to escape, he was there to open it for her.

Elaine had gone to the bookroom alert to the need for haste, aware that Mr Woolford was expecting the arrival of a client. It was only the second day she had been allowed downstairs following her collapse at The Griffin and she was still shaky. She had just taken up a large volume of hand-coloured flower illustrations when, to her dismay, she heard someone enter the room beyond the archway. She turned as swiftly as she dared on the library steps, hoping to see only Mr Woolford, but the man who walked into view was a stranger. This, she supposed, was the expected client, Mr Cato Raffen.

There was nothing immediately remarkable about him; nothing in particular to hold her rooted except her quivering awareness that he stood between her and an easy escape. A year or two past thirty possibly, he was moderately tall, compact of figure and quietly dressed in a blue-grey coat, fawn buckskins and top-boots. His thick dark hair, still compressed by the hat he had obviously recently removed, clung about a well-shaped head and his skin was of a browner tone than the English climate usually imparted.

She prayed he would continue past the archway to look out of one of the windows; that would give her opportunity to be down the steps and out of the room before he knew she was there.

Instead, his head lifted and, swift as a striking snake, he swung towards her. As though his gaze had impaled her, she found herself incapable of moving, yet when he walked through the archway to the bottom of the steps, it was in so normal a manner as to make her paralysis ridiculous.

He looked up at her with eyes that were curiously both dark grey yet bright, and which seemed to hold a faintly ironic humour. Everything about him spoke of self-assurance and self-sufficiency; the inverse of her own present nervous weakness. She felt threatened. Men like this were altogether outside her experience. Mr Woolford she did not count: his four visits a year to Great-aunt Sarah had made him familiar, even a friend . . . an unhappy child's kind, undaunting and only friend.

All her concentration on controlling the infuriating trembling of her limbs, she looked down at the hand extended to take the book she was clutching. It was the lurking amusement in his eyes when she looked into them again that had at last goaded her into thrusting the book at him and finding enough command of herself to get down the steps without falling and take back the book.

Filled with a bubbling resentment, she now sat by the fire in the small parlour, the book unopened on her lap. Just why she felt so strong a resentment towards Mr Cato Raffen she was not entirely sure. His arrival had been ill-timed and he had appeared to be laughing at her . . . but was that really enough to put him on a par in her mind with her cousin, Oliver Marney? No, she decided, not *quite* on a par. Her one and only meeting with Oliver must surely stand alone.

She had no recollection of how that particular occasion had ended. Her last memory of it was of a desperate need to escape, to find somewhere where she could draw air into her suffocating lungs. After that there was nothing until she woke to the warmth and comfort of a strange bed and found Mrs Woolford – pretty, managing, good-hearted Fanny Woolford bending over her.

That marked the beginning of the second time her life had taken a dizzying change – but this time so very much for the better. So why sit here fuming over a brief encounter with a man she was never likely to see again and a cousin she was clearly better off without? What she should be doing was looking ahead in the pleasant knowledge that, at nineteen, she was a rich woman and her own mistress.

The thought revived an almost forgotten zest for life, set free the first real flow of returning vitality. As a child, before she had been whirled out of all that was familiar into Sarah Marney's hostile orbit, she had often longed to take a look at the wide world, longed to spread her wings. . . .

Her green eyes lit as her spirit leapt up to embrace the fact that now she could.

Four days later Elaine discovered that even from the grave Sarah reached out a hand to lay upon her future.

Discussing the terms of Sarah Marney's will with her to ensure she understood them, John Woolford read aloud again the clause that stated:

. . .I devise and bequeath all else of my property both real and personal whatsoever and wheresoever situate unto my great-niece Elaine Luce Marney . . .

Plain enough. The sting came in the continuation:

until marriage so that she may be provided for in her single state. Subject thereto I give devise and bequeath all my real and personal property to my great-nephew Oliver Marney absolutely

'In other words,' the lawyer said gently, 'if you marry, on that day, Miss Marney's fortune passes from you to Mr Oliver Marney. I'm afraid there is no hiding the fact that your great-aunt wished you to remain single, as she did. The law does not allow for marriage to be expressly forbidden you, but in effect, that is the likely result of what she has done. I speak plainly, Miss Elaine, because in my experience it is always best to face facts if there is to be any hope of turning them to advantage.'

His smile was meant to comfort and encourage her but suspecting that what she saw in his face was compassion, she waited in wary silence.

'What it is important to remember,' the lawyer went on quickly, 'is that you can now look forward to a life of comfort, security and independence such as few single young women enjoy. And though a woman's hopes naturally centre on having a husband and perhaps children, one should remember, too, that not every woman is given the opportunity to marry.'

'You are saying, I think, that without the recommendation of a fortune, I am unlikely to receive a proposal of marriage?'

It was what he had meant. Looking at Elaine Marney as she sat before him, haggard and shadow thin, without a worthwhile dowry, what hope could she have of any man proposing? But he would have preferred not to have his meaning phrased so bluntly.

'I am advising you to be cautious in your expectations,' he said carefully. 'Lack of fortune must always be seen as a major obstacle to a young lady marrying because any sensible man considering taking that important step must consider whether his income is sufficient to support a wife and family. Not infrequently, the lady's dowry is what makes it possible. And though it is true that upon occasions men allow other . . . er . . . factors to cloud their judgement, the result can be disastrous. A penurious marriage destroys happiness.'

What was painfully clear to Elaine was that Mr Woolford saw

her as entirely lacking in feminine charm – as her cousin Oliver had done – and so was trying to guide her into being content to stay rich and single and to forget dreams that were impossible of fulfilment.

She said nothing to suggest she rejected his counsel, but under her apparent acceptance a slow fire of rebellion began to burn . . . .

CHAPTER THREE

*C*ato Raffen's visit to Bellehaugh, the Woolfords' home had been well timed because winter's freaks had not ended with the fog.

A few days after the visit the snow began, floating down, innocently white, innocently gentle, to mantle the landscape. But as it continued, hour on hour, drifts piled tree-high in an increasingly blind, white, soundless world.

The Cambridge Mail Coach, bravely attempting a journey, was snowed up and completely covered for eight hours. Fourteen heavy wagon-horses were needed to drag it out with its passengers nearly frozen to death. No coal was to be had except in the vicinities of the coal-pits and the Thames froze sufficiently for a frost fair to be held on it. It was 5 February before a thaw came, to be followed, inevitably, by floods.

The three Woolford boys, all at Winchester School, spent Christmas where they were like many other similarly stranded and unhappy scholars throughout the land. Elaine, secure in the comfort of Bellehaugh, thought of what such a winter would have meant had she and Sarah still been living as they had and could not believe they would have survived it.

A warm friendship had sprung up between Fanny Woolford and herself despite the seventeen years' difference in their ages.

Fanny, impatient of formality, soon insisted on first names being used between them and, when the weather relented at last, refused to allow Elaine even to think of leaving.

Highgate was briskly astir after the long weeks of enforced social inactivity. Invitations, flowing in every direction, were eagerly accepted even by those who had to face the steepness of Highgate Hill and the readiness of its surface to turn to glutinous mud.

By April, Elaine began to feel herself an experienced socializer. Her health recovered, the worst of the uncomfortable shyness of the early days had passed. Now, handsomely gowned, the good manners her gentle mother had instilled in her remembered, she was finding herself at ease among the Woolfords' friends and acquaintance.

The end of March had brought the best of reasons for a party – the end of the seemingly endless war with France. France had asked for a truce and Napoleon had abdicated. Victory bells rocked steeples throughout the land when, on the 11th April, Easter Monday, a treaty was signed with the Allied Powers.

The party the Woolfords were to give on the 20th however, had as much utilitarian purpose as pleasure in its aim, the guests chiefly being drawn from among the valuable, but less distinguished of John Woolford's clients.

Elaine joined Fanny in the drawing-room before the first guest had arrived and was greeted with smiling approval. 'That green velvet is *most* becoming but I fear it will be largely wasted on the solid citizens who are our guests tonight. Still their respectability gives rise to the hope that none will succumb to the influence of wine before dinner is at an end. The servants have difficulty removing recumbent bodies from beneath the table with the same neatness they remove the roast from its surface. And if one leaves an offender there, they invariably *snore!*'

Surveying the staid assembly from a fern-sheltered vantage

point some time later, Elaine saw little promise of such diversions. There were two more guests to come however, and the first of these arrived in the next five minutes: a tall, handsome young man, fair haired, blue-eyed, bright-faced, impeccably stylish in his evening dress. Before long, Fanny brought him to meet Elaine.

'This is Jeremy Lazelle, my sister's nephew by marriage,' Fanny told her. 'He manages to do nothing useful with great spirit. . . . And no, Jeremy, you may not remain to talk to Miss Marney just yet. You are here to leaven the lump as I warned you. And your immediate task is to charm the look of terror from the Mellishes' young daughter whose first venture into society this is, so I understand. Heaven alone knows why her mama should choose it for the poor child!'

Jeremy followed Fanny with good grace, yet it seemed to Elaine that his eyes promised an early return. It could be no more than a polite gesture, she told herself, but it had been charmingly done.

As she sank down on to the small sofa behind her to finish the glass of Tokay she held, a door to her right opened and the last guest entered.

Recognition sent a tremor along her nerves. It was the man she had encountered in John Woolford's bookroom, Mr Cato Raffen. Brief as that meeting had been, it lived strongly in her memory. Now, like a revived essence, something of the disquiet she had felt then rose up in her again. She had known that John Woolford had invited a last-minute guest, but she had not known who it was to be.

Through the curving fronds of fern she watched Raffen take a further two steps into the room and stand collectedly, his gaze seeking his host and hostess. Now as before, she could see nothing remarkable in his appearance. And yet . . . and yet. . . . *Something* there was that marked him as different. Something, she thought a little wildly, that seemed to hint that behind Mr

31

Raffen's outward quietness there was a man of singular unquietness. A hunting tiger, crouched among long grasses to watch his unsuspecting prey, might have just such an air as his. . . .

Between a laugh and a shiver she tried to dismiss what could only be an overstrained fancy. Yet she could not drag her attention away from the man. The bones of his face stroked fine, clean lines under smooth flesh, not quite as deeply brown as she remembered it . . . a face that, though not easily seen as handsome, drew the eye back for a second look. Some might well think him attractive, but Elaine, remembering with discomfort the devil of sly, provoking humour that had once looked out at her from his darkly grey eyes, could not find him so. It was all too probable, she thought, that Mr Cato Raffen harboured other devils even less attractive to her.

At that moment he turned and took a step in her direction. It was unlikely he had seen her, but even as she prepared to retreat, Jeremy Lazelle reappeared before her.

'Tell me, Miss Marney, why it is we have only just met? Where have you been hiding until now?' he demanded.

Elaine looked up at him in smiling relief. *He was here to leaven the lump*, Fanny had said. Given the beguiling combination of marked good looks, ease and charm, he would hardly need to exert himself. He was probably an accomplished flirt, but if he was choosing to flirt with her just now, Elaine intended to enjoy it.

Tilting her head to smile up at him, her green eyes sparkling, she gave him back his own coin. 'As the nursery song says, *"Daffy-down-dilly is new come to town"*.'

The blue eyes glinted amusement. 'I remember my sisters singing that. There's something about a *"yellow petticoat and a green gown"*? I see the gown but must imagine the petticoat. Still, it's very well met, Miss Marney, even if I wish it could have been sooner.'

32

At a small distance, John Woolford, pausing to glance over his guests, caught the quintessential moment of their exchange and was shaken. Was that really Elaine Marney? She had been living in his house and under his eye for four months – how could he have failed to see the magnitude of the change in her?

He knew he was not an imaginative man and recognized the reason was that he had not foreseen it. The change had come about gradually while he had continued to carry in his mind's eye, the image of the gaunt, drained, charmless creature she had been. Of course, he had been aware her appearance had improved, but what he was seeing now was transformation.

It was not that Elaine Marney had suddenly become a great beauty; more disturbing even than that, what she now possessed was a dangerous allure. It was implicit in the twist of her head on her slender neck, the slanted eyes, the bewitching curve of her mouth in a face that though still triangular in outline, had had its sharp points tenderly rounded. His gaze swept over the rest of her. Gauntness had been transformed to lily-stem slenderness but with curves beguiling enough to rouse the Old Adam in any man.

Arriving at her husband's elbow to whisper that dinner would be served in the next few minutes, Fanny's gaze travelled to find the fixed focus of his. With smiling satisfaction, she said, 'Who would have thought a few months ago that Elaine would come to such bloom.'

'Who, indeed!' John Woolford agreed sombrely. 'But placed as she is, I fear it is far from being in her best interest.'

'Oh, no! How can you say so!' Fanny opened indignant hazel eyes on him.

'Very easily, given the terms of her great-aunt's will and men being what they are. I saw her former lack of attraction as a safe-guard that would allow her to settle securely into enjoying the pleasures of a good income without being disquieted by hopes that must fail of fulfilment. After the misery of more than eight years of virtual enslavement by that obsessed old woman, my wish is to see her *safe*. Looking at her now, Fan, I fear for her, as I would fear for a daughter of my own if similarly placed.'

'But why should her improved looks be a danger to her? It is the very thing to advance her hope of finding a husband.' Fanny flashed a mischievous smile up at her own pleasant-faced but serious husband and gave him back his own words: '*Men being what they are.*'

John Woolford remained sombre. 'Because, my dear, as she is now, she must appear an absolute honeyfall to any man looking for a well-endowed wife. And if such a one pays court, perhaps wins her heart, and then learns her fortune vanishes on marriage, it is more than possible he may seek to enjoy the woman even if the fortune is beyond his grasp. What then, Fan?'

'But all men are not such villains!'

'Men are often driven by compulsions not easily understood by women.'

Fanny frowned. 'Well, she cannot return to looking as she did. Nor can we change the way she thinks and feels. After those dreadful years with her great-aunt, she wants to enjoy what the world has to offer and she has no wish to live with a dull companion and a snuffly little dog. She hopes for a home and husband and I am determined she shall have her chance to find them. Somewhere there must be a man of sufficient substance who would be pleased to marry her and care nothing for her lack of fortune.'

'But no certainty of their meeting, Fan. And you well know how rigidly the boundaries of society are kept. Who among our own friends, aware that her father had been nothing more than the master of a small school, would do as much as bow to her in the street? I think we may have been wrong in introducing her to our acquaintance . . . wrong in giving her entry to a world in which she can have no permanent place.'

34

Looking down at his small, plump and pretty wife, he added dryly, 'Do you think I don't know that it is only because *you* are the daughter of Baron Dalton of Wintershall and sister to the Countess of Sheffney that I, a man of trade, enter those of the great houses that I do?' Diverted for a moment by wry remembrance, he said, 'Even now, after so many years, I suspect I am a long way from knowing just how you brought your parents to consent to your marrying such a man.'

Fanny, remembering very well, shot him another mischievous smile. 'I shall not flatter you into unbecoming smugness. If you are content that we married, be content that they *did*!' More seriously, she added, 'But I cannot agree with all you say concerning Elaine. Our friends accept her. She is at ease among them.'

'But if marriage were in question you would find them a great deal more inquisitive.'

'John, she *must* have her chance! I shall find a way.'

John Woolford's frown deepened. 'Beware of what you do, Fan. Look at your sister's nephew-in-law at this moment and remember he is a second son with expensive tastes who lives in hopes of attracting a wife with a comfortable fortune.'

'Jeremy can be hinted away. He's not without sense,' Fanny dismissed airily, her eyes gleaming with the light of inspiration. 'But you have reminded me. . . . My sister! Dear Giddy Gertie is the very person to find Elaine a husband. Neither of her daughters are great beauties yet see how well she has married them both. With Sheffney in Paris, Cecilia still on her wedding tour and Helen carried off to Scotland by her husband, Gertie must be at quite a stand for what to do next.'

With a hint of exasperation, John Woolford said, 'Have you heard anything I've said, Fan? Even if Lady Barlborough were willing – which I doubt – she would be launching the girl into deeper waters than we have done.'

But Fanny, aglow with purpose, dismissed that with a wave of her hand. 'You are too cautious, John. If Gertie will do it, you may be sure she won't let Elaine sink. She knows her world . . . knows to the last point the worth of those around her, both as to fortune and character.'

'I'm aware that if *giddy* were ever an apt description of the countess, it is not so now. Your sister has admirable good sense.' Woolford's tone was dry. 'But I cannot—'

A discreet cough interrupted him.

'All is ready for dinner to be served, madam,' said the manservant at Fanny's elbow.

Elaine, entering the dining-room on Jeremy Lazelle's arm, was disappointed to be separated from him. Fanny had taken some part of her husband's warning to heart and, with the excuse of the late inclusion of an extra guest, had made a lightning change in her intended seating arrangement. Consequently, Elaine found herself directed to a seat between Mr MacGregor, a naval lieutenant, and an empty chair.

A minute or two passed before anyone approached the vacant place. Looking round then, Elaine was given a bow and an unrecognizing smile by the least welcome dinner partner Fanny could have found for her among the present company – Mr Cato Raffen.

She counted herself fortunate that Mrs Grislander – a large lady with a superfluity of diamonds about her person – immediately laid a seemingly unremitting claim to Cato Raffen's attention.

In general, the chief topics of conversation were provided by the news daily filtering across the channel and the many plans in preparation for celebrating the peace. Linked with those was the day's gossip concerning Louis XVIII, *le desire* of his people and a king now and so no longer merely the Comte de Lisle. Louis, having dragged his poor old gouty self to the Abercorn Arms at Stanmore, had been met there by the Regent and a number of the nobility wearing the white Bourbon favours in his honour. Later, in a procession of suitable pomp, he had been carried on to London, first to meet the Duchess of Oldenburg, the czar's sister, and then to face a public reception. Rumour had it that he had almost collapsed from exhaustion before the reception began. Opinion added that meeting the duchess – already famous for her rudeness, her quizzical appearance and her general 'busyness' – was sufficient in itself to exhaust anyone. Threaded through all was the name of the man who for years had sown death and destruction throughout Europe, but now spoken with less awe than it had once commanded.

'I am told,' a male voice rumbled weightily above the rest, 'that Napoleon was pushed into abdication only when told by the French Government that it was *his* war and *France* intended to make peace. It is said he attempted suicide the day after signing the treaty, but bungled it by using a poison that had lost its efficacy and so suffered no worse than a bad bellyache.'

' "*Ingratitude, more strong than traitors' arms, quite vanquished him . . .*" ' quoted Jeremy who was seated on the other side of the table a little to Elaine's left. His laughing gaze netted hers and he went on, 'But it was not, I think, "*the most unkindest cut of all*". That, surely, was to have been deserted by his valet – somewhat inaptly named *Constant* – who, in going, robbed him of a hundred thousand francs.'

Inadvertently, Mrs Grislander relaxed her grip on Cato's attention for a moment and he at once turned to Elaine. He had counted himself at least half lucky when he had come to table and seen who were to be his neighbours. Even before the girl had turned, his interested gaze had admired the long, pale, graceful neck that supported a head of charmingly dressed golden-tawny hair. Nor had he been disappointed when she looked round at him. The broad brow, long, lovely eyes and a mouth both tenderly and temptingly curved above a delicate chin, made up a

face with a piquancy he found more engaging than mere pretti-
ness.

He had seen, too, the sparkling smile with which she had
acknowledged his fellow-guest's anecdote. Hoping to be similarly
rewarded, he took up the theme, bending towards her to say, 'It's
a sad fact that while some sympathy may be found for an
emperor abandoned by his countrymen, an emperor abandoned
by his valet can only be seen as ridiculous.'

His voice had the deep undertones and the odd vibrancy Elaine
remembered too well. Though she had known that the moment
must come when he would turn to her, she was still unready for
it. She had wondered if he would recognize her and what his
reaction would be if he did. So far, it seemed, he had not made
the connection. More stiffly than she intended, she said, 'So it
would appear, sir.'

He had won neither sparkle nor smile. Piqued, Cato persevered. 'I arrived too late to be introduced, but as we are seated
side by side an introduction was clearly intended. Allow me to
present myself: my name is Cato Raffen.'

The look he gave her was open, his smile attractive, his devils
in abeyance. Elaine bowed and murmured her name.

Wondering if her smiles were reserved exclusively for the young-
man-about-town on the other side of the table, Cato felt the first
faint tug of memory. Had he seen her before? If he had, surely he
would not have forgotten her. . . . Taking up the popular topic
again, he said, 'I have heard that though Napoleon has not yet
sailed to his exile in Elba, already it is being whispered in France
that Papa Violette will return in the spring with the violets. Not a
comforting thought do you think, Miss Marney? Or are you one of
the surprising number of his admirers to be found here in England?'

Before she could answer, Mrs Grislander's commanding voice
brought a new topic to general attention.

'One may hope that when the present frenzy of excitement is

at an end, the government will direct its attention to the unrest among the common people. It is said to have to do with the price of bread, but how can that be when so much is given away in Poor Relief? It is my opinion the common labourer will always prefer to drink and riot about rather than work, so there is small wonder if he is needy. Only last week—'

What else the lady had to say was lost in the bustle attending the introduction of the second remove. Cato turned to Elaine again.

'Do you share the lady's view that the poor need not be so if they did not choose to be, Miss Marney?'

The near-pauperism Elaine had shared with Sarah had opened her eyes to that of others around them in the miserable alley in which they had lived and to the diversity of its causes.

'I think the poor have few, if any, choices. What, generally, they most need is a means of helping themselves.'

Did Miss Marney's responses have to be quite so bleakly unhelpful, he wondered. Perhaps she belonged to the Methodist persuasion? He appraised her appearance more carefully. Though her only ornament was a gold chain and a simple golden ribbon was all that ornamented her hair, her gown was expensively fashionable and set off her delectable figure in a quite fascinating way. There was nothing in the least indecorous about it, but neither did it suggest a primly self-conscious modesty.

Perhaps she had merely parroted someone else's views? She both intrigued and annoyed him. The lilt of her voice, threaded with quiet laughter, had charmed his ear when she had spoken to the naval officer on her other side. What had Cato Raffen done to be so differently treated?

A gleam in his eye and a laugh in his voice, he asked, 'But you would not have the poor help themselves to the possessions of others? You would not actively *encourage* burglary?'

Memory of the very real pains of hunger coloured Elaine's

answer. 'But if I were a man and my family starving, I might not think burglary such a crime!'

Her words had been intended for his ears alone, but they fell into a momentary silence and several astonished and disapproving looks were turned on her. Elaine flushed with vexation.

Her tormentor raised mocking eyebrows. 'What dangerous ideas you entertain, Miss Marney. But suppose *you* were the one robbed?'

'I hope I should judge the circumstances understandingly,' she said with a snap.

The gleam in the granite-grey eyes brightened to a devilish glint. 'A pious creed, but a difficult one to follow. You cannot believe all rogues merely unfortunate?'

'No. Nor do I believe all unfortunates merely rogues.'

He laughed. 'Axiomatic but most unpopular! Am I allowed to ask the source of your alarming radicalism?'

Recklessly and through her teeth, Elaine replied, 'Entirely the natural harvest of experience, Mr Raffen.'

His laughter this time was a sharp crack of disbelief. 'I suspected you were leading me on: now I know it!'

She had piled error on error, Elaine knew. It was past time to let the infelicitous conversation drop, but as though impelled, she flatly contradicted him. 'In that, sir, you are altogether wrong!'

The green blaze of her eyes – so clearly consigning him to the devil – catapulted Cato into recognition. Unbelievably, this was the shabby, starveling creature he had scooped up from the floor of The Griffin, and the same speechless piece of vacuity he had encountered in Woolford's bookroom. Surprise held him silent while he adjusted his ideas. Hers, it appeared, was a rags to riches story from which had emerged a sharp-edged, provocative Cinderella no longer speechless. His curiosity deepened. But where was the sweetness, the vulnerability he had thought he detected when he had first looked down at her unconscious face?

40

Before either could speak again a servant came between them offering a dish of Madeira ham and Mrs Grislander renewed her claim on Cato's attention with an imperative grip on his arm.

Left to reflect on their conversation, Elaine's feeling of guilt increased. Had she needed to be quite so defensive? So humourlessly intense? Their first meeting was now hazy in her mind and she could not recall exactly what it was that had planted such a deep and lasting distrust in her. But even if she had failed to be the most charming of dinner partners, she did not think he would suffer long through it – everything about him spoke of hardy self-sufficiency. She sighed. If only Fanny had placed her next to Jeremy Lazelle, how much more enjoyable this endless meal would have been.

The cloth was drawn and desserts set in place: Elaine took a few nuts on to her plate. As she picked up a nutcracker it was taken from her by Cato Raffen.

'Allow me to be of service.'

He spoke without any hint of ruffled feelings and guilt stabbed her again. She could not complain of any lack of civility on his part. Watching his lean brown hands put an almond between the jaws of the nutcracker, Elaine saw that the back of his left hand was marred by an ugly puckered scar partially hidden by the pleated cuff of his shirt. It was strange looking wound and she wondered how he had come by it.

The opened almond now revealed a double kernel and the small snicker of sound Raffen made in his throat as he extended the shell halfway between them alerted her to mischief. His tone however was utterly bland, as he asked, 'Will you allow me to share your philippina, Miss Marney?'

Having no idea what he meant, she said, 'You are welcome to it all.'

'But I should so much rather share. . . .'

She mistrusted his smile, but took one of the twin nuts and

watched with sceptical eyes as he bowed and tucked the remaining nut into his fob pocket. The small parade thrust her deeper into irritation and she longed for Fanny to rise from her chair.

CHAPTER FOUR

*T*wo days after the dinner-party Fanny was gratified to receive a visit from her elder sister, Lady Barlborough, Countess of Sheffney. The sobriquet Giddy Gertie had attached to her in her youthful and adventurously inventive years, but it was only in her family that it still clung to her.

Dressed in high fashion, Her Ladyship sailed into Fanny's drawing-room, established that Fanny was alone and without more ado, demanded, '*Who*, Fan, is the green-eyed enchantress who has Jeremy waxing lyrical in a manner he usually reserves for his horses?'

'Oh dear!' said Fanny, laying down the book she was reading and rising to accept her sister's kiss.

'Oh dear, indeed!' said Gertie with a keen look. 'Unless she has sufficient fortune to keep Sheffney's nephew in the state in which he and his horses prefer to be kept.'

'You are speaking, I must suppose, of Elaine Marney about whom I told you before you went off to Gloucester. Her fortune, I regret to say, vanishes the day she marries,' Fanny returned baldly.

'*That* you could not have told me. Can you mean it?' Gertie paused in the act of folding her tall, elegant figure down on to the other end of the sofa her small plump sister had occupied.

Completing the action, she sighed. 'I see you do. How does such an extraordinarily Gothic arrangement come about?'

Fanny gave her a brief outline of the terms of Sarah Marney's will, then, with her usual impulsiveness, plunged on, 'Your coming is particularly well timed for you are the very person I have in mind to frustrate the old woman's unkind intentions. I've grown very fond of the girl, Gertie. She spent eight years of her girlhood in the most miserable circumstances and deserves better than to find herself condemned to spinsterhood at nineteen years of age. *You*, I am sure, can easily find her a husband . . . a pleasing sort of man with sufficient fortune of his own not to need a wife with a dowry.'

Gertie laughed derisively. 'Ever the romantic, Fan! *Easily* I could not. Think how many there are on the scramble for such a man. As for attempting to introduce the daughter of a schoolmaster into society – my dear, you know that's nonsense. The girl herself would be miserable, I'm sure.'

'Dukes and earls have married actresses and cooks before now,' Fanny returned undaunted. 'And Elaine is not absolutely unconnected. Her maternal grandfather was a Roding. A younger son of a younger son, but still a Roding. He was rector of a parish centred on the village of Cheveney Cresset in Dorset.'

'Then it is the Rodings' business to sponsor her.'

Fanny frowned. 'John made application for their interest soon after Elaine was sent to live with her great-aunt. She was a child, not eleven years old, yet they would do nothing for her. The rector's marriage, though perfectly respectable, had been deeply disapproved for some reason, and was still hugely resented.'

'Then there is nothing to be done, Fan. And if, as Jeremy appears to think, she is a walking temptation, to set her among the rakes of the ton would be no kindness to the girl. Merely to survive, she would need a clearer head and a hardier spirit than most girls of nineteen possess.'

44

Fanny threw her hands wide in appeal. 'She has them both, Gertie. Truly she has! And I have set my heart on Cinderella going to the ball. All I ask is that you put her in the way of meeting a Prince Charming. You and I have been so uncommon lucky in our marriages, I feel we have almost an obligation to help someone so unhappily circumstanced.' Her eyes narrowed mischievously. 'Besides, you cannot have not grown so tame as to refuse the challenge. Where is the giddy girl who danced three times widdershins round our old effigy of Pan in the wilderness? At dawn on May morning, barefoot, in nothing but your shift and you a great girl of fifteen!'

'And you a provoking ten-year-old busybody to come creeping after me as you did.'

Her Ladyship spoke without rancour, her gaze drifting into distance and a small reminiscent smile curving her lips. 'It doesn't seem so long ago, yet here am I forty-one years old with two married daughters.' She sighed and brought her gaze back to Fanny. 'Oh Fan! It really did seem as though Pan worked his ancient magic when I met Sheffney for the first time that very evening and we were at once both so sure we were destined for each other. We never wavered, did we, though we had to wait two years to marry.'

Fanny laughed. 'As well for you Pan worked quickly because you had a red nose throughout the week following that first meeting from the cold you took. Had Sheffney seen you then, he would have been frightened off forever.'

Gertie's gaze, bright hazel like Fanny's own, sharpened combatively. Fanny held up a placating hand. '*Dearest* Gertie,' she coaxed, 'I am convinced that anything Pan can do, you can, if you only *will*. And I have another reason for asking: soon I shall be unable to take Elaine about because I am increasing.'

'Fan! Why did you not say at the beginning! After ten years, too! Is all well? Are you pleased?'

'Oh, yes, all's well and certainly I'm pleased because this time I *know* it will be a girl.'

'When will it be? Have you told John?'

'November. About the middle, I think. And, yes, John knows.'

'Well, take good care of yourself. I will take Miss Marney off your hands and find her a husband if I can, though not, I think among the ton. For that she would need exceptional quality and a reasonable dowry. You know it is so. I shall do my best for her, I promise, but I shall know how best to go about it when I have seen her and can judge her quality. Meanwhile, I trust you have not filled her with hope of high romance, Fan. An older man . . . a widower with a young family in need of a mother . . . something in that way might be achieved. But I make no promises. . . .'

The result of Elaine's meeting with the Countess of Sheffney exceeded Fanny's hopes.

'Better than I would have thought possible. She shall have her chance and we'll see what comes of it,' the countess had observed privately to her sister.

Urging Elaine to accept Her Ladyship's invitation, Fanny had said, 'My sister would welcome your company because her husband has been absent longer than either he or she expected. It will be a great thing for you, too. An adventure. I know you long for a home of your own and to achieve that, you must hope to marry. London is the best of all places and the likeliest for a young woman in need of a husband to find one. And this year, with Napoleon vanquished, London will be the gayest place in the world.'

Aware of Fanny's pregnancy and that she needed to live a quieter life, Elaine had yielded to the double persuasion and within the week the countess's travelling chaise had carried her from Highgate to Berkeley Square.

She had experienced her first real misgiving as soon as she stepped across the threshold and began to realize the true magnitude of the step she had taken. Fanny's home was luxurious by any standard she had previously known, but it had not prepared her for the sheer, daunting grandeur of Gertie's London house.

Now, just three weeks later, standing a step behind the countess, it appeared to Elaine that the whole self-assured, imperious world of rank and fashion was flowing up the elegant stairway of Sheffney House to attend Gertie's first grand ball of the season and her own translation to this glittering sphere seemed more unbelievable than ever.

Every now and then the countess drew Elaine forward to be presented to someone selected from the colourful, bejewelled tide.

'Those to whom I shall introduce you on this occasion will be my trusted friends,' Gertie had told her, and Elaine did her best to store away names and rank against any subsequent meeting and prayed harder than ever that the rules and skills she had learned in the past three weeks would take her safely through the social maze she was entering.

'High style, courage and good humour will usually carry the day,' Gertie had told her. 'Let no one put you out of countenance. If nothing else will do, raise your eyebrows, look astonished and pass on. You have it in you to do it well.'

Elaine hoped Her Ladyship was right, but could not help remembering John Woolford's troubled reserve when he had been told of the proposed move.

The number of arriving guests was beginning to thin when she saw Jeremy Lazelle's shining golden head rising among the rest. Jeremy in dress regimentals was a sight to dazzle any female and her heart gave a small lurch. They had met a number of times since the night of the Woolfords' dinner-party and his open admiration had continued to boost her confidence so undermined by John Woolford's assessment of her sad lack of feminine charm. For that alone, Jeremy must always have a place in her heart. Yet it was through him that she had been given her first lesson in the reality of the handicap Sarah had imposed on her.

'There can be no future in Jeremy's attentions, my dear,' Gertie had warned her. 'Like you, he has to marry where there is money. As a younger son his income is comparatively small and he keeps within it with the greatest difficulty. He, too, has been warned of the unwisdom of allowing a lasting attachment developing between you. Look on him only as a useful escort to be called on when needed.'

Jeremy turned from greeting his aunt-in-law and regarded Elaine with a shadow of rueful consciousness in his eyes.

Gertie said smoothly, 'I expect you are longing to dance, so go with Jeremy now, my dear.' Then in a lower tone, murmured, 'Remember, I rely on both of you to be sensible.'

As they walked into the brilliance and splendour of the ballroom, Jeremy's admiring glance flowed from Elaine's now fashionably cropped curls crowned by a chaplet of silken ivy leaves and pearls, down over her gown of white embroidered gauze covering an underslip of pale, sharp green.

With a shake of his head, he said, 'Being sensible holds no attraction for me.'

'But is none-the-less necessary.' Elaine gave him a slanting smile.

Gertie's warnings, coming so early in their acquaintance, had somehow launched them into a degree of openness impossible to have achieved so quickly in normal circumstances.

'I cannot help but think of what might have been.'

The dogged note in his voice gave Elaine some unease and trying to lighten his mood, she said teasingly, 'Ah, but that may not have turned out as you suppose. In six months, six weeks, six days even, you – we – may see matters quite differently. It is the way of things.'

'I do not believe it. I shall continue to hope for a miracle.' On that intransigent note he swept Elaine towards the sets forming for the next dance.

It did not surprise Elaine that Jeremy danced superbly well and she was thankful to be able to feel she had not disgraced herself. When they rejoined Gertie who had now come into the ballroom, Jeremy, half challengingly, claimed the right to partner Elaine for the supper-dance. Gertie flicked an irritated glance at him but did not give the matter importance by making a demur.

As her dance-card filled, Elaine's fear that no one but Jeremy would ask her to dance disappeared. Her confidence had grown to the point of being able to view Mr Raffen's unexpected approach with reasonable equanimity. He had been a late arrival and Elaine had been dancing when he first sought out Gertie. When he came up to her again, it was between dances and Elaine was at her side.

He and the countess spoke together with a familiarity that suggested a long and friendly intimacy before Raffen turned to Elaine and said, 'So we meet again, Miss Marney.'

Elaine inclined her head in acknowledgement and Gertie, glancing between them, said, 'You have met before?'

'Three times but have not yet achieved a formal introduction,' Cato told her.

'Then let me remedy that.' Gertie turned to Elaine. 'Miss Marney may I present Mr Raffen, an old friend too long absent from this country. Cato . . . Miss Marney who is kind enough to give me her company while Sheffney remains abroad.'

Curtsying to Cato's bow, Elaine said, 'We have met but twice before, sir, surely?'

'I stand corrected. We have met twice before.' He gave her a glinting smile.

It seemed to Elaine he had put a small emphasis on the word *met* and she wondered what he could have been implying.

He did not remain with them long, nor did he ask Elaine to dance for which she was both thankful and piqued.

Gertie sighed as he walked away. 'Poor Cato! He is as unfortunate in his family as you have been in yours. It is why he has been so long abroad and why – though he is his brother's heir – he does not use his proper patronym. Raffen is merely *one* of the family names.' She glanced at Elaine. 'I suppose you met him while you were with Fanny? It was I who sent him to consult John. Even inheriting a small estate from an elderly cousin has not been the unmixed good fortune it might have been for him. The estate is in a poor way and there is a dispute over boundaries. Arguing the matter may prove more costly than the property is worth. It is all so defeating. Cato is, alas, another poor man in need of a rich wife.'

Mr Raffen had been making his way past a nearby group that included several young people but had been halted by a pretty young girl who put out a hand to detain him and draw him into her group.

Watching the lively, laughing exchange between the two that followed, Gertie drew a pleased breath. 'Ah! Now that is an acquaintance Cato would do well to pursue.' Lowering her voice a little she confided, 'The young lady is Miss Pilford who is heir to her maternal grandfather's fortune said to be immense. To her great credit she is also said to be a very amiable young woman.' A little later, returning from a visit to the ladies retiring room, a refreshing stir of air from a open window made Elaine pause and move deeper into the angled recess to breathe in the welcome coolness. Staring out into the shadowed garden, her thoughts drifted. She had enjoyed the evening more than she had expected: no dragons had crossed her path; partners had appeared in complimentary numbers and most had been both pleasant and good dancers.

She recalled her dance with Lieutenant Dacier with particular pleasure. A Frenchman and ex-prisoner of war, his manners were charming and he had been interesting to talk to. He had told her that, having given his parole, he had been allowed to reside in a private residence in the small country town of Odiham in Hampshire. He had spoken amusingly and without rancour of being allowed to travel only a mile from his billet and only on a main road; of the boredom arising from a lack of intelligent amusement, congenial company, and an early curfew. But, he had confessed, he was more fortunate than most of his compatriots in having funds available in this country. Free now to go where he chose, he was staying with Lord Stapford with whom he had family connections.

Her thoughts turned to Jeremy. Dear Jeremy! Her sigh was more sentimental than deeply felt. The initial tug of attraction was still there, but it had not taken her long to realize the wisdom of Gertie's warning. The London season for the young unmarrieds had more to do with the matching of fortunes and status than hearts and wishes: love-matches such as Gertie and Fanny had made were not the rule and she realized that a match between Jeremy and herself was unlikely ever to have been countenanced. She hoped Jeremy's show of reluctance to accept the warning they had been given was more chivalrous than real. For her part, she was determined not to be the cause of any upset in Gertie's family.

Fanny had been right, she *did* long for a home and someone with whom she could share it in warm affection. Since that needs be a husband, she added her own unspoken prayer that he might be gifted with kindness and a capacity for laughter. What Gertie had said to her was that it would be sensible to look for a *comfortable* man – comfortable in fortune and temperament. It had been a warning not to indulge in extravagant dreams, that her situation required her to use her common sense.

It shook her to discover at this moment that common sense is a bitter herb. She turned to glance over the the crowded ballroom and wondered rebelliously if there was not a man present tonight who could love her, dowerless as she was, and whom she could love in return.

It was folly, she knew, to let the thought take root as a hope and she thrust it out of her mind. But hope is a deceitful weed well able to flourish in secret under the shade of carefully nurtured prudence.

The window by which she stood was recessed and set at an angle created by some long-ago structural alteration. Turning again, she found herself looking into a small antechamber that was little more than a short wide passage. Colourful tapestries clothed the walls and two coramandel cabinets held exquisite porcelain. An ornate candle lantern in the Chinese style gave light. Two men stood beneath the lantern in earnest conversation. One, Elaine saw, was the ubiquitous Mr Raffen; the other, an older man, was as dark as Jeremy was fair. The simple and elegant perfection of his attire and his air of almost princely command were enough in themselves to fix attention. The fact that he was also the most handsome man she had ever seen was something of an overplus.

Suddenly, the two men nodded as though in agreement and began moving briskly towards her. She took a hasty step back into her niche and as they were both still talking, hoped to avoid notice. At the last moment, however, Mr Raffen saw her and gave her a smiling bow before passing on. The older man's glance swept idly over her, checked, became a stare. In another moment, recollecting himself, with a bow of apology, he, too, walked on.

For several moments, Elaine stared after them then, recollecting that a partner would by now be waiting for her, she hurried to find Gertie.

Elaine had just joined the dancers with her latest partner and Gertie was about to stroll among her guests once more, when she was halted by a voice she knew well saying over her shoulder, 'Tell me Gertie, who is your charming young friend?'

'James!' Gertie acknowledged as the man walked into view. 'I suppose you to mean Miss Marney.'

'Miss Marney,' he repeated softly. 'Not a common name.' He turned a thoughtful gaze on the dancers, looked back and said quizzically, 'So I have her name. Am I permitted to know more?'

'What more do you wish to know?'

'Just the usual.' His smile, darkly, coolly brilliant, teased her. 'Where she sprang from . . . what her connections are . . . what her fortune is?'

Gertie raised astonished eyebrows at him. 'James, there is nothing usual in your wishing to know such details concerning a girl of nineteen. What am I to think?'

'Whatever you choose. An onset of senility, perhaps . . . age beginning its preoccupation with youth?'

'Nonsense! You are exactly the same age as I am.'

'I'm sure you malign yourself, my dear. Looking at you, I cannot believe it.'

'You don't have to – you know my age as well as I know it myself.'

'But how ungallant I would be to admit it! But why so slow to explain Miss Marney? Is there a dark secret attaching to her?'

Gertie gathered her wits and replied airily, 'Great heavens, no! She is the ward of a dear friend and is staying with me for a few weeks.'

'Which friend?'

Startled by both the question and its tone, Gertie's eyebrows rose more sharply upward. 'How very uncivil of you, my lord! Now I begin to question your interest in earnest.'

'And I am no longer *James*! Believing myself acquainted with all your friends, I am surprised to learn that one of them has a ward of nineteen of whom I have never heard.'

James Eldred Luce Valdoe, Marquis of Braxted, had been her husband's close friend since boyhood and Gertie since her marriage had seen a great deal of him. She liked him and their relationship was friendly, but it had never developed a depth to match that which existed between the two men. She met his dark-eyed, intelligent gaze and suddenly uneasy, lied again. 'I doubt you are acquainted with this one for she is an old schoolfellow who does not leave her country home.'

'Has Miss Marney *no* connections with whom I am acquainted?'

'Not unless you know any of the Rodings. Her grandfather was a Christopher Roding.'

'As it chances, I have slight acquaintance with the family. Enough to know they also never leave their country home. How very ill the young lady appears to have chosen her kith and kin.'

His interest in Elaine had taken Gertie by surprise. It was out of character and she was unable to decide whether or not he was teasing her. She said a little crossly, 'It makes little difference. Because of a family disappointment over Christopher's marriage, they refuse to recognize her.' She gave him a sharp look. 'You must admit, James, it is beyond being wonderful for you to show interest in a girl of nineteen.'

'With no pretence at modesty I would expect your response to be nearer delight than wonder. So why isn't it, Gertie?'

More certain now that he was laughing at her, Gertie rallied her defences. 'Because, James, I have a responsibility to see Miss Marney's head is not turned by too overwhelming a success too soon. Drawing the attention of so eligible – so *confirmed* – a bachelor as the Marquis of Braxted on her very first appearance in society, can only be regarded with alarm.'

His eyes gleamed wickedly back at her. Softly, mockingly, he said, 'I find this a most instructive conversation, my dear. Do you suspect me of having developed rakish tendencies? And we such old acquaintance!'

'Think as you choose, James! But if all this roundaboutation is simply leading to a request for an introduction, for heaven's sake say so.'

His smile told her nothing. 'Not immediately, my dear, so you may sleep easy tonight.' He took one of her hands in his and raised it to his lips. 'Dear Gertie, forgive me. It is quite an experience to have raised a small flutter in the dovecot of your good sense. Just now I am come simply to make my adieux and give thanks for a most entertaining evening. I leave early only because I am bidden to Carlton House and His Royal Highness does not care to be kept waiting. However. . . .' – he held the pause for perhaps five seconds – 'I shall hope for the pleasure of an introduction to Miss Marney on another occasion.'

A bow, another enigmatic smile and he was gone.

CHAPTER FIVE

For the miles travelled, Cato thought tiredly, as he turned his mount into the lane leading to Ringlestones, the information gathered amounted to very little and proved less.

He would have declined the request to interest himself in the matter had it come from any other source than it had, or concerned any other than the Prince Regent himself. Those things being so, choice had been removed. But it was not for *this* that he had returned to England. He was ten years out of touch with the mood and make-up of its people, of its politics and even of the physical changes in the country itself – disadvantages he had already felt. With a little luck though, he would discover before too long that there was nothing behind the warning given to the prince of an attempt to be made on his life. It had been given directly to him by a lady the prince had refused to name. Misplaced chivalry, so Cato considered. It was fortunate that Braxted had been able to present him privately with a choice of three, of which the second to come under his scrutiny had provided a starting point for his enquiries through the medium of one of her grooms. He was still left with the prospect of some part of the journey he had just made having to be repeated and extended to the coast. His hope was that that might be the end of it, with proof found that the threat had faded away or never had any reality.

The narrow, overgrown lane led nowhere but to the gates of Ringlestones, the unexpected inheritance that had brought him back to England. The ground was less rutted than that of lanes in more general use and he slackened rein to allow the tired grey to choose its own pace. Overhead the arching trees met and interlaced excluding the last glimmering light remaining in the late evening sky, but the darkly shadowed aisle ended just before reaching the gate-piers where the drive to the house began, the pale stones of which Cato could now see. The gates were not in view, being held open by a sturdy growth of grass and weeds. There was plenty yet to be attended to before he put the place on the market, he thought. Thank God enough had been done in the house he was making a temporary home, to offer hope of some comfort when he reached it.

Off guard, he was aware of movement a moment too late to ward off the weighty black shadow that launched itself from among the crowding bushes on the left-hand bank. Weight and surprise combined to allow him to be hauled out of the saddle and fall heavily to the ground. He fell on his back and was given no time to recover the breath thumped from his lungs before his assailant had straddled his body and falling to his knees, used his weight to clamp him to the earth.

A fleeting glitter of light down a long lifted blade shocked awake the instinct for self-preservation and Cato drove a fist as hard as his supine position allowed into the exposed midriff. Breath grunted out of the man and he bent, but the knife continued down still with force. Hampered though he was by the restricting weight, Cato twisted wildly aside. The blade missed its target by a handspan to drive instead through the flesh of his inner arm. In the second before it was yanked out to be used again, Cato clamped his hands about his assailant's wrist and put the strength of desperation into twisting it in an unnatural direction. Desperation opposed by savage determination created

deadlock. But his life the prize, Cato had the greater incentive
and he again wrenched viciously at the knife-wielding arm. This
time the man rolled with the twist of his arm, most of his weight
lifting from Cato to be transferred to his right knee. Held now
only by the leg still stretched across him, Cato stiffened his body
and heaved with all his might.

He achieved more than he had dared hope for. As more
weight was thrown on the man's right knee, it skewed and gave
way and he fell heavily on to their linked arms. As he did so, he
emitted a long gurgling sigh, his body convulsed and lay still.
Cato waited for a cautious moment or two before releasing his
grip on his attacker's wrist and dragging his arms free. Getting
to his feet, he felt the after-tremble of extreme effort. His hands,
he saw, were darkly smeared. He stood for a moment flexing
stiff fingers and breathing deeply, then bent single-handed to
heave the man on to his back. He had fallen on his own broad-
bladed knife which, entering his throat at a low angle, must have
severed both inner and outer jugular veins before emerging on
the right.

It was too dark to see any obvious reason for the way the
man's leg had collapsed . . . perhaps the shift of position had
brought a sharp edged flint under his knee, or perhaps it had
been due to some old injury. Whatever the cause, Cato was
thankful for it.

He stood in thought for several minutes. The place for ambush
had been well chosen given the man could not have had much
time to choose. Robbery had never been the object: the whole
intention had been murder and could only be connected with the
search he had begun. Which meant there was substance in the
matter. Only a short time ago he had decided it was not what he
wanted, but now, like a hound that hears the horn and lifts his
head to scent the adventurous air, he found mood and attitude
had changed. His enquiries had been low-key and discreet, but

they had clearly poked a stick into a wasps' nest. The speed of the response suggested an identity for the dead man and opened wide the question of whether he had been able to pass on the knowledge that had brought him here to anyone else. Time and events would provide the answer but that he would need to be vigilant was obvious.

Meanwhile, it was necessary to move the body and to give some attention to his own injury. Blood was running down his arm still and he was aware of it becoming more painful and weaker. He needed help, and that could only come from Ringlestones.

That in itself was a problem. What staff he had there was recently acquired and temporary. The only male he employed was Adam Kerby, his groom. Twenty-six years old, not above middle height but sturdily built, he was strong enough to be useful and no fool. What, though, of the man himself? Sparing of words, his face gave little away. He had lost his last employment through the sudden death of his bachelor master for whom he had worked for seven years. His reference had come from his master's lawyer who knew the master better than the man. The most valuable part of the recommendation given was that the groom would not have been so long retained if he had not given satisfaction.

In the three months he had been employed at Ringlestones, Cato had found him both competent and conscientious. But it was not enough to tell him whether he could rely on the man's co-operation in the present situation and on being sure of him keeping his mouth firmly shut afterwards. Again, he was left without choice. Kerby it would have to be.

As though summoned, Kerby was already on his way.

Scenting blood, the grey Cato had been riding had snorted disgust and jigged away between the gates. There he had paused briefly to look back at his owner just pulling himself up from the ground, but after a long day, the comforts and nearness of his stable had proved irresistible and he headed for them at a smart trot.

Adam Kerby had heard the clop of shod hooves on the cobbles of the stable yard and come out of his quarters next to the stables to survey his riderless charge's return with surprise. He lit a lantern, stabled the animal, removed saddle-bags, valise and saddle and forked hay into the manger but made no start on grooming. Leaving the stables, he walked round to the front of the house. There was no sign that the master of the house had arrived, no light in any window. Yet the horse had not given the appearance of having been long parted from its rider. He set off down the drive, not knowing what he expected to find, if indeed, there was anything to find so close to home.

It was the intermittent scrunching of Kerby's footsteps alighting on the patchy gravel of the neglected drive that alerted Cato to the groom's approach, the man himself just recognizable in the remaining faint luminosity beyond the trees. He stooped to draw the knife from the dead man's throat and having wiped it clean on the grass verge, he stood with the knife held loosely in his right hand waiting for Kerby to reach him.

The groom looked briefly at the pale blur of his employer's face then down at the black on black, unmoving and unmistakable shape at his feet. 'He's dead, sir?'

'Yes.' Cato gave him a bald outline of the circumstances.

Kerby threw a glance up at the sky. 'It's late.' Short as the remark was it conveyed the opinion that the nearest magistrate was at some distance and would have no liking for being called out at this hour. There was no suggestion that he, Kerby, was reluctant to be to sent on the errand, though he added, 'Haven't attended to the grey yet, sir, only unsaddled him. He's tired.'

'Yes,' Cato said again, agreeing that the grey had priority. 'But we have to put this fellow under cover for the night. There must be a horse somewhere. He didn't walk here.'

'I'll take a look around.'

Kerby moved off and Cato occupied himself kicking loose earth over the blood that had spilled from the man's throat. He had died quickly and the flow had soon stopped.

He was making a tired assessment of what the future might now hold for him when Kerby loomed out of the darkness leading a small, sturdy horse.

'Tethered short in the meadow next to the potato field. Cropped all the grass within reach,' Kerby told him.

'Right. Let's get this fellow across his back.'

The horse, less particular than the grey, stood unresenting while it was done. Cato was aware of Kerby taking more than his share of the weight. Even so, he was also aware of a fuller flow of wet warmth from his injury afterwards.

With Kerby leading the burdened horse, they walked in silence along the drive until branching off as though by common consent into a track leading directly to the stables. There, Cato asked, 'Does the household know I'm back?'

'No. Subahdar came straight to the stables. They're all abed in the house. Mrs Stretton has the three lasses up betimes.'

'No need for them to be told anything then. The tack-room has a key, hasn't it? We'll put our silent friend in there.'

They carried the dead man past the six stalls into the room which lay at the end and laid it on the boarded floor where it could not be seen from the window or glimpsed through the doorway. Kerby brought the lantern through and they stood looking down at the man.

'A seaman, I'd say,' Kerby offered.

'Yes. The clothes and the ear-rings suggest it.' And seemed to confirm the man's identity but still left open the question of what he might have told anyone else. Cato bent and went through the man's pockets. They yielded nothing but what might be expected to be found in an ordinary seaman's pockets, except for the rather large number of coins in his sock-purse. The sturdy quality of his clothing was the best of its kind and though it showed wear here and there, nothing was in need of being replaced. A seaman then, who did unusually well out of his occupation: what could he be but a smuggler?

Looking up at his stolidly waiting groom, Cato wondered what questions were foremost in his mind. He said, 'Can you put up with having him as your companion for twenty-four hours? Perhaps even a little longer? I can offer no explanations yet, but when I can, I will. Will that content you for the time being? And can I rely on you keeping your mouth tight shut at all times? You will not be running yourself into trouble, I assure you. But for that you have only my word.'

'I'm not one for gabbing, sir.' Kerby stared woodenly back at Cato and seemed to think he had said enough. Then, as a last minute rider, he added, 'As I see it, he was waiting for you, not you for him.'

'Just so. Cover him with that horse-blanket hanging behind you then, and we'll leave him here. Lock the door and remember to keep it locked.'

That done, Kerby carried the lantern back to its hook above the stalls and said imperturbably, 'I'll see to Subahdar now, shall I? And the one in the yard?'

'Yes. Stable him, too. I'll decide what's to be done with him in the morning. There's one more thing tonight: I've seen you doctor a horse – can you do something of the kind for me?'

It appeared Kerby had already taken in the darkened area on the sleeve of his mulberry riding coat and his bloodied hand, because these were the areas at which he at once looked. 'Depends how bad,' he said laconically.

'I doubt I'll die of it. But see to the horses first. I'll get myself out of my coat and shirt meanwhile.'

Kerby looked as though he was about to argue, but changed his mind and said only, 'Use my room if you will, sir. There's a fire there. The door's open.'

Cato went out into the yard and in through the door on the left of the stable block. Kerby's quarters were just one sizeable room with a large closet leading off it. The living-room had an ancient box-bed closed in by panelling, a modern iron range that gave off a comfortable glow and plain country-made furniture providing two upright chairs, a table and a chest for storage besides the two cupboards either side of the range. Another older chair, broadly built and cushioned and with a look of having seen better times, offered comfort close to the range. The stone walls were match-boarded to half their height and white-washed above. The close-packed brick floor was clean and dry, with the cheerful addition of a colourful rag rug before the cushioned chair.

Removing jacket and shirt was a slow, unpleasant business, Cato found. He had lost a fair amount of blood and was glad to sit quietly in the cushioned chair afterwards with the shirt bunched between his arm and his body to soak up any new flow of blood, his coat draped over his shoulders for warmth. Tiredness came in on a full tide and he must have dozed for Kerby seemed to appear both soon and suddenly. Having eased the shirt from under Cato's arm, he frowned and said, 'No lasting damage done, but it'll need a stitch or two.'

'Well, do what you think necessary.'

'You did ought to see a proper doctor after.'

'If I need to. Just clean me up for now and do what you think.'

'You'd best take a drink before I get to the stitching. I've only rum.'

'It will do.'

He swallowed what Kerby offered him in a pewter mug and nodded to him to begin. The tender flesh of his underarm quivered under the groom's ministrations but between the rum and

what he had learned in India he came through wincingly but without disgrace. Bandaged with a clean neckcloth from the valise
which Kerby had brought through and dressed in a clean shirt
from the same source, he leaned back in the chair, relieved to
have the ordeal over.

'Give me ten minutes. Then I'll let myself into the house and
get myself to bed. Thank God I don't have a valet to ask awkward
questions!'

Kerby occupied himself tidying away the evidence of his neat-
handed doctoring. When Cato was ready to leave, he went with
him carrying the valise. There, with the ancient oak door opened
by a weighty iron key, Cato took the valise, saying, 'Can you burn
the shirt and jacket tomorrow without exciting anyone's interest?'

'For certain, sir.'

'And you'll be sure to keep the tack-room door locked?'

'That's even more certain.'

Cato heard the faintly sardonic note in his voice and laughed
appreciatively. 'You're a good man to have at hand in a crisis,
Kerby. I owe you thanks.'

Kerby nodded embarrassed acceptance, said a hurried
'Goodnight, sir,' and walked away into the night.

There was more to Kerby than his stolid appearance
suggested, Cato reflected thankfully, as he climbed the stairs to
his room with the slow care made necessary by the weight of rum
he carried, loss of blood and sheer weariness. But most of all by
his anxiety not to wake his household of women.

CHAPTER SIX

*I*n the week following Gertie's ball, there had been many visitors to Sheffney House, but two weeks passed before they saw Cato Raffen again. He came about four in the afternoon and Gertie immediately gave instructions that she was no longer 'at home' to other callers.

Gertie greeted him with the kind of affectionate familiarity usually reserved for a favourite brother and, sitting relaxed in her chair, said, 'I've seen too little of you since your return, Cato, and so it is from Sally Jersey I learn that you took a heavy fall from your horse three days ago. Are you quite recovered?'

'How Lady Jersey should have learnt of it I have no way of knowing. But apart from a little stiffness in the left arm and a bruise or two nothing remains of it to signify.'

'And if anything does you would not admit to it. As well I know. So tell me instead if there is there any forward movement in the matter of your cousin's estate?'

'As far as I know John Woolford now has some hope of convincing the intruder and his friends of the falsity of the claim before the matter comes to court. Whether he really can do so still remains to be seen.'

Turning to Elaine, Gertie explained, 'For some time, a neighbour has been extending his activities across a neglected boundary of a property Mr Raffen has inherited. The man is laying claim to a substantial part of the land. It's an ancient property and the documentation is less clear than it might be.' She turned back to Cato. 'If he is persuadable, John will do it. It will save you a deal of expense. If only it might be quicker! It is time you had a suitable residence, Cato, and Richmond is very conveniently placed for coming into London. It is time, too, you took your place in society and looked round for a wife.'

Cato gave her a crooked smile. 'I cannot agree. It is too late for the first, too soon for the last.'

She sighed and shook her head at him. 'You are a sad case, my friend. Did you go to Eldenshaw as you planned? Is there any change there?'

'I went and there is change – but nothing to please. I should have done better to have stayed away. But do not let us speak of that. Allow me tell you I have the honour to be dining this evening with an interesting friend of yours, the Marquis of Braxted.'

Her last encounter with the marquis still fresh in her mind, Gertie said a little shortly, 'Certainly he is interesting and his manners are charming. I cannot say he is liked by everyone, but he and Sheffney have been friends since boyhood. But when and how did you meet?'

'He introduced himself to me at your ball. On a recommendation from Castlereagh. And we met again very briefly two days ago.' Something in his voice suggested he had found that meeting amusing.

Gertie's gaze had sharpened. 'For a purpose? Yes, of course! Put together the foreign secretary, Braxted and *you* and it has to do with the Prince Regent. I am right, am I not?'

He grinned at her. 'Very possibly.' He glanced towards Elaine. 'But my affairs cannot be of interest to Miss Marney.'

Gertie smiled an apology at Elaine. 'Miss Marney will forgive me, if I steal a few moments more to satisfy myself that an old

friend has not allowed himself to be persuaded into an unreward-
ing venture as has happened on too many other occasions.'

Elaine had been wondering how to withdraw without discourtesy and took this as a good opportunity. She stood up. 'I will
leave you to talk while I—'

As though her action had woken a mischievous perversity in
him, Cato, rising too, threw out a detaining hand. 'Do not go,
Miss Marney, I beg. The countess slanders me. In reality, I am the
least persuadable of men. Besides there is nothing more I can tell
Her Ladyship at this time and I have a proposal I should like to
put before you.'

Elaine sat down again, not pleased to have her escape cut off
and vaguely disquieted by the distant echo of laughter in his voice.

With the privileged insistence of an old friend, Gertie said, 'If
you are dealing with Castlereagh and Braxted you could find
yourself in the jaws of a nutcracker. Castlereagh is single-minded
in his service to his country and Braxted is devoted to the
Regent's interests. Assure me, Cato, you are not committed to
another rash undertaking.'

He grinned at her again. 'Rash I never am!'

'Are you not! Do you think Sheffney has not told me of some
of your exploits? Shall I now question your self-knowledge, or
your truth?'

' "What is truth said jesting Pilate; and would not stay for
an answer." As I shall not.' He stood up, crossed swiftly to
Gertie as she also rose, and taking one of her hands in his,
touched it briefly with his lips. 'You must know your continuing
kindness through the years has been a bright star in a sometimes very dark heaven,' he said softly. 'But remember I am
older and wiser now, my dear, dear Gertie. The scars I gathered
in India will keep me prudent. Or nearly so.' He smiled into her
anxious eyes.

Gertie continued to look anxious. 'It troubles me that you have already risked so much for little gain. That there is no beat of drum, no public recognition of what you have done.'

He laughed. '*That* is something to be thankful for! Think how Wellington suffers from it, hating it as he does. And the poor man is destined to suffer a great deal more when he returns to this country.' His eyes gleamed and were hidden. 'And my years in India were not entirely without reward.'

Elaine had been only half attending to what was passing between the other two but the notion suddenly flared into her mind that Cato Raffen was a spy. And a spy, as anyone who read the newssheets must learn, was a creature without honour, trading in treachery, vile. Somewhere she had read that just to be seen in conversation with a known spy was to attract greater disgrace than to be seen in the company of the public hangman.

Cato turned to her at this moment and with uncanny insight caught the essence of her thought. She saw it and blushed.

With a sharp desire to punish, Cato bowed ironically. 'Just so, Miss Marney,' he said with suave malice. 'Did I not tell you I am a travelling man? But do not regard it for the moment. You may think as badly of me as you choose another day. Now I am on the side of the angels and wish to propose an airing in Hyde Park. Trust me thus far, I implore you. By now, my servant should have returned my phaeton to the door and if you will agree and Lady Barlborough will permit, it will be my pleasure to drive you there. The countess will vouch for my behaviour in public and for my being a reliable whip.'

Gertie glanced questioningly from one to the other and Elaine knew she was trapped. This was Gertie's friend and she was a guest in Gertie's house: she might frame an excuse that Mr Raffen would be forced to accept but Gertie would know it to be false.

Misunderstanding her hesitation, Gertie said reassuringly, 'To be seen driving in the park at the fashionable hour is obligatory, my dear. So put on your smartest bonnet and allow Mr Raffen to show you another of society's curious customs.'

Seething with annoyance, Elaine curtsied acceptance and went upstairs to put on her outdoor things. What pleasure could Mr Raffen hope to gain from an unwilling companion? He had behaved in a perfectly correct manner when last they met, but now. . . . How was she to endure being caged with him in a moving vehicle for whatever period he chose to keep her there?

To her further annoyance, there was an unmistakable glitter of triumph about him when she joined him, though he veiled it with attentive courtesies as he escorted her down to the street and into the waiting vehicle. But she had herself in hand now, and she met it all with icy grace.

Poor Mr Raffen might be, but it was a very elegant phaeton that awaited them. Olive-green in colour, it was drawn by a pair of light bays harnessed in tandem. The groom holding the head of the lead horse was given leave for an hour which told Elaine the length of her penance. Surprising her, the groom questioned his master's decision, saying on a curious note, 'Do you mean to drive yourself, sir?'

'I do.' The tone in which the man was answered, though quite good-humoured, was too decisive to be questioned further and Elaine was left to wonder if Mr Raffen's recovery from his fall was quite so complete as he claimed. It was only a short distance from Berkeley Square to Hyde Park but with the influx of visitors to the capital to see the celebratory sights, traffic was heavy and conversation necessarily limited. As her irritation abated, Elaine had time to reflect that she had no right to judge the means by which Cato Raffen made his living. Gertie had said he was a poor man and she, herself, should know to what straits those without money could be driven. She found it curious that Gertie appeared to honour him. Had she made a mistake? The reasons for her own jaundiced view of him were not entirely clear in her mind.

71

All she could be sure of was that her meeting with him in John Woolford's library had left a deeply unfavourable impression on her; an impression that had been strengthened at Fanny and John Woolford's dinner-party. Something in him seemed to threaten her peace, made her uncomfortable in his company.

Five o'clock being the hour of the fashionable squeeze, the park was as crowded as the streets. It seemed that all who could be there, were, on foot, on horseback or in one of a variety of carriages. A few came for air and exercise, but, as Mr Raffen told her, the greater number came to see the gallanty-show and take their part in it.

Cato, too, had had time for reflection. He valued Gertie's friendship too highly to put it at risk by causing an open rift with Miss Marney. He well knew the dangers of acting on impulse, yet that was what he had done in inviting her to come with him on this drive. And why? Because she had ruffled his plumage, offended his masculine self-esteem. Now, because of the deliberate provocation he had given her, he must find a way to charm her out of her retreat into gelid civility and establish some kind of harmony between them before they returned to Sheffney House. It meant restraining his recurring urge to tease her: an urge he had not troubled to trace to its source. He slid a sideways glance at her interesting profile and wondered if she could be brought to bestow on him the quite captivating smile he had seen her award other men.

The sights to be seen in the park provided plentiful material for conversation and Elaine's first view of a particular middle-aged couple sauntering along dressed in the last extreme of fashion drew an audible gasp from her. The woman's cerise gown showed quite six inches of embroidered stocking above her ankles, her deep-fringed shawl was multi-coloured and her enormous bonnet bore a Dunsinane forest of nodding plumes. The man's tight, long-tailed coat had near saucer-sized buttons while his trousers, made in the cossack style recently originated by Lord

Petersham, were so full and so long it was a wonder he was not tripped by them.

'Those,' Cato told her, 'are prime examples of a dandy and a dandizette. In particular they are Sir Percival Oxwold and his lady. Known to the irreverent as The Fizgigs.'

'How can they bear to make themselves such figures of fun!' said Elaine.

' *"To see and be seen, in heaps they run"*,' quoted Raffen.

' *"Some to undo, and some to be undone"*,' Elaine laughingly capped, her reserve forgotten.

He looked at her with surprise. 'Dryden?' he said. But it was not the source of the quotation he was querying.

'Dryden's translation of Ovid. I was well-taught in my early years, Mr Raffen.' She turned a look of demure mischief on him as she spoke.

'Indeed!' he agreed, frowning at her with deepening curiosity. Taught well beyond what was usual for females, too. And this was the young woman he had once thought simple-minded!

'My father was a Greek and Latin scholar and a schoolmaster. Until he died, I learned with the boys he taught.'

Her antipathy forgotten, she smiled at him, her green eyes gleaming from under the brim of her delightfully rakish Wellington hat. Had her father's death been the calamity that had reduced her to the dreadful level in which he had first seen her, he wondered? And in how many more ways could she yet surprise him?

'Lady Barlborough mentioned you were orphaned at an early age,' he prompted hopefully.

The brightness faded from her face. 'Both my parents died at the same time. Of the cholera,' she told him flatly. 'I was a few months' short of my eleventh birthday and I was sent to live with my great-aunt, the only relative who could be discovered.'

Her tone told him that removal had been a far from happy

one. 'A sad difference for you, no doubt,' he offered quietly.

'Yes.' With an effort she cast off the shadow and changed the subject. 'What of yourself, Mr Raffen? I am told you have been in India. The little I know of that country suggests it to be both desperately hot and desperately strange. I cannot think I should like it.'

'I think perhaps you might, though its fascination is not easily explained. It is a country where time and space seem to blend into a single dimension which, by its immensity, reduces the individual to a grain of sand in a desert of eternity. The Indian accepts that reduction with patience and humility, but we, the English, mostly find such acceptance beyond us.' He paused, his gaze bridging distance, then on an almost caressing note, he said, 'It is a country where great beauty, wisdom, riches and marvels exist side by side with great ugliness, ignorance, poverty and barbarity. You could liken it to a circus: by day, gaudy, noisy, odorous, vulgar and – to the knowledgeable – cruel, but at night, under a dazzle of flares, quite magical, the dross transmuted to shining gold! By like contrasts, India is unforgettable!'

An inexpertly driven curricle snatched away his attention. The sudden movement necessary to avoid collision, threw Elaine against his left side. She felt him wince, heard his short, sharp intake of breath and thought that his fall had caused more damage than he had admitted to. She found herself at that moment gazing down at the hands whose quick, confident management had averted a collision. Their lean elegance made the disfiguring scar on the back of his left hand all the more noticeable.

His gaze followed hers and he said with a grin, 'An ugly-looking paw, is it not? One of my less pleasant mementos of India, but I am well content to have kept it in my possession. The army doctor to whom I presented it as a raw and ragged mess told me there was no alternative to lopping it off – preferably at the elbow. I thanked him for his opinion and took myself off to an old Indian fakir with a reputation for healing to whom I indicated my attachment to my extremity. What he put into his pastes and infusions I never dared to ask, but they worked the cure. He also taught me something of the mystery of controlling pain, a very useful piece of learning.'

'But how did you come by the injury in the first place?'

The brand of laughter that was peculiarly his own, flared in his eyes. 'Ah! That was a small matter of expediency in the face of a shortage of rope and my being unwilling to remain where I was. There is, alas, a surfeit of bandits in India, and I had met with one who was in a particular hurry at the time. The quick solution to his problem was to pin me to a tree.'

'*Pin!*'

Her look and tone of horror amused him. 'With a bare bodkin, Miss Marney. A dagger. I could not complain. He could as easily have skewered me to the tree with a sword through my middle. But it chanced that we had met before and had shared a few jokes and so he inclined towards magnanimity. It was my misfortune that when his men had caused me to be thrown from my horse, I had dislocated my right shoulder, which made releasing myself from my predicament an exquisitely painful and messy business.' He grinned at her. 'But as you see, I am still in one piece, whereas the bandit chief lost his head little more than three weeks later. Quite literally. A sword removed it.' His eyes narrowed on her in his unholiest smile. 'Now, Miss Marney, what are you thinking? That mine was the hand that wielded it?'

The look she gave him met mischief with mischief. 'Lack of opportunity, Mr Raffen?'

'What else?' He bowed acknowledgement, his brown vital face alight with self-mockery. 'How well you read me!'

They were leaving the park now, and it occurred to him that

against all the odds and without the effort he had expected to have to expend, they had found a very pleasing rapport.

Reaching Sheffney House he handed the reins to his waiting groom and accompanied Elaine into the house. There they exchanged thanks, she for an interesting drive, he for the pleasure of her company. Both spoke with sincerity.

Cato turned to say goodbye to Gertie. Because for some unexplored reason he was feeling pleased with himself, in a moment of exuberance, he winked at her. His back was to Elaine and he was unaware of facing the mirror into which Elaine was looking.

She saw the wink clearly and at once the pleasure of the afternoon was destroyed. Her distrust of him took on new life. The man was a trickster . . . a huckster in an infamous trade who had amused himself for a while gulling foolish Miss Marney into a state of absurd complacency. She should have known better!

She would not make the same mistake twice, she told herself furiously. Within the bounds of necessary courtesy to Gertie's friend, in future he would get nothing from her but the contempt he deserved.

CHAPTER SEVEN

*E*arly in June, the Czar of Russia, the King of Prussia and a large company of other notables arrived in London to be entertained throughout the next three weeks to an unremitting succession of banquets, reviews, concerts and parties both public and private. When on the 27th of the month the crowned heads departed and their retinues departed, they left behind the hardiest and most popular of the visitors, General Blücher, who, in the absence of the Duke of Wellington, was regarded as the lion of lions.

Continuing the sequence of celebrations, hostesses were shameless in the wiles they used to capture this particular luminary, but failing him, hunted down with equal determination two or more lesser lights to shine in his place. And if an excuse was needed for extravagance, it could be claimed that with prices tumbling down – sugar by as much as thirty shillings a hundredweight, brandy sunk to 4s.10d. a gallon, burgundy two shillings a bottle and claret only a shilling – giving a party might be thought almost an economy.

There was no uncertainty about General Blücher attending the ball to be given by the Duchess of Richmond and the word went round that the Regent had given notice he might 'look in', which was his way of signifying his probable attendance.

Elaine had ceased to wonder by what alchemy Gertie achieved the inclusion of her unimportant house-guest on such occasions and was looking forward to having a closer view of the duchess's two most distinguished guests. She had also been hoping to meet Fanny and John Woolford, but Fanny's pregnancy was proving troublesome and they had been obliged to cry off at the last minute.

The one place to which Gertie had not attempted to introduce her protégée was Almacks. She agreed, she said, with the subterranean opinion that the lady patronesses were despots and she would not invite refusal. Besides, the place provided dull entertainment and duller refreshments. It mattered nothing to Elaine. From what else she had heard of it, she thought it an unlikely place in which to find the kind of husband to whom she might aspire.

That kind, Gertie had hinted, might well be a slightly older man, perhaps widowed, with no need to consider rank or fortune. But Fanny and Gertie had both married men they loved, Gertie making a brilliant match, Fanny stepping down into trade. Both were still happy with their choice. It was their freedom of choice that Elaine found enviable. . . .

Jeremy was on duty tonight and unable to come, but Lieutenant Léon Dacier, the young Frenchman whom he had introduced at Gertie's ball made early application for a dance. A year or two older than Jeremy, without being handsome, he was an attractive young man with a thin, intelligent face and something in it that hinted at a not unadmirable pride and a capacity for passionate feeling. A very French Frenchman, Elaine thought with a small, amused, tolerant smile. For all that, though repatriation of the 72,000 prisoners of war was already under way, Dacier appeared happy to prolong his stay in England with his English relations, Lord and Lady Stapford.

The Marquis of Braxted, arriving late, very soon sought out

Gertie and laid claim to an introduction to Elaine. He followed it with invitation to dance which Elaine was free to accept. Watching heads turn as the two went to join one of the sets, Gertie found some of her vague apprehensions reawakening. To have attracted Braxted's notice was a heady success for any girl, but for one in Elaine's circumstances it could prove positively dangerous.

Remembering the startled stare he had turned on her once, Elaine met the marquis with interest. She was struck again by how very handsome he was. Time had touched him lightly; there was no grey visible in his crow-black hair and his figure remained youthfully slim and pliant. The few lines the years had graven on his face were those of character rather than age, but not a character easy to read.

Conversation between them in the pauses between the figures of the dance was pleasantly easy. Asked if she was enjoying her first season in London, Elaine told him, 'As much as most girls, I imagine. That is, I am in constant passage between terror and delight.'

'Terror?'

'Of making some dreadful mistake.'

'What dreadful mistake could you possibly make?'

'It is simply not knowing that, that creates the terror. Wondering if some hideous unsuspected pitfall lies in wait for me.' She smiled up at him as she spoke and realized that his dark eyes were not brown, as she had supposed, but a deep, slatey blue.

'And what delights you?' he asked.

'Almost everything . . . balls like this, parties, picnics, musical concerts, the libraries. . . . I have little discrimination as yet. And there is one mistake: enthusiasm is not at all fashionable, I'm told.'

'It's refreshing to find. You have lived quietly in the country until recently, I understand. In Somerset?'

'Somerset? No.' She looked her surprise.

'The Rodings live in Somerset. Are you not connected with them?'

She knew Gertie thought it an advantage that her connection to the Roding family should be known, but Elaine was nervous of claiming a relationship about which she knew so little. With flat honesty she said, 'My mother's father was a Roding but I never knew him. Nor does the family acknowledge me. My father was a schoolmaster.'

If His Lordship was in any way shocked to find himself dancing with the daughter of a mere pedagogue he showed no sign of it, and if he wondered at her passage from her father's narrow world to the plutocracy of Gertie's he did not question it. Smiling down at her, he merely said, 'You have come to London in a most exceptional year. Have you met any of the heroes of the hour?'

'Indeed I have! Only a short time ago, I was introduced to General Blücher. He shook my hand. But I believe it to have been a mistake, for I fear he was not quite sober at the time.'

'He rarely is!'

She gave him an impish look. 'Nor are half the gentlemen of England by ten of the evening, though I should not say so.'

'No, Miss Marney, you should not.' He laughed as he spoke and there was no disapprobation in his words.

'Whom I had hoped to see at close hand tonight was our own Prince Regent, but he has not yet come.'

'Nor will, I think. His time is not always at his own disposal.'

'I find it extraordinary that so much adulation has been lavished on visiting notables and so little prominence given to *him*.'

'It is the Regent's misfortune to have become alienated from his own people. He has faults, but the Press has loaded him with more discredit than one man could well earn in a lifetime. The commonalty take Blücher to their hearts for all his uncouth, peasant manners, but the Prince's courtesy is as deliberately disregarded as his other and greater virtues.' This was plain speaking and partisan for all that he spoke with dry dispassion.

It was their turn then to go down the dance. When it finished and they returned to Gertie, with the merest hint of mockery in his tone, the marquis told her, 'Here is Miss Marney safely returned to you, you see.' Giving her no time to respond to that he turned to Elaine, thanked her for her company and added, 'It was a pleasure I hope you will allow me to repeat before too long.' And with that, he moved away.

Frowning, Gertie stared after him. What was his interest in Elaine? It would be wonderful indeed, if having failed to find a young woman to suit him among the prettiest and most eligible he should find himself captivated by Elaine Marney. But would he marry her?

He was no monk, Gertie knew. He had a mistress in keeping, a discreet liaison because it was not in James's nature to parade his private arrangements. The Valdoes had always been known as a proud race and she found it difficult to believe that any Valdoe could bring himself to consider marriage with a girl of such doubtful ancestry as Elaine. But he had said he would seek Elaine's company again and James did not toss off idle remarks of that kind. . . .

In fact, no more than three days passed before Braxted called at Sheffney House to request the pleasure of Miss Marney's company on a drive to Hyde Park. The marquis could not be refused and a nod from Gertie told Elaine she might accept. She did so with her usual composed grace and left the room to put on her bonnet.

Gertie regarded her visitor with severity. 'What are you about, James? When did you last take a girl of nineteen driving in the park?'

'A pleasure too long neglected, perhaps,' he said suavely. 'Though the ladies I *have* driven there have been some years from their dotage, Gertie, my dear.'

'But generally they have been older, married women who have seen it as a compliment merely. As society has seen it.'

'Is it less a compliment to Miss Marney?'

'No; it is more. It will raise a great deal of speculation. Miss Marney does not have a secure place in society. She is vulnerable.'

'Can you be asking what my intentions are after one dance and an invitation to drive in the Park? A little premature, surely? And at present, I have none of which I am certain.'

'All the more reason to give thought to what you do . . . to consider the disparity of rank, fortune and experience between yourself and Miss Marney. The Rodings do not acknowledge her. Fanny, John and myself are all the friends she has in the world.'

'A powerful enough triumvirate for her protection, I should have thought.' His gaze teased her. 'Have you considered that Miss Marney may have it in her power to do *me* harm?'

Gertie stared at him for a moment before dismissing this with an impatient, 'When the Devil is blind, James!'

Something flashed in the dark depth of his eyes, but then he smiled sardonically and said, 'Do I appear so dead to the tender emotions? How interesting it is to learn in what light one's friends see one.' His gaze lingered meditatively on her for a moment or two before he said, 'Shall we dispense with the story of Miss Marney being the ward of an old friend living in the country? And will you tell me why the Countess of Sheffney is sponsoring the daughter of a schoolmaster?'

Gertie hesitated. She knew no ill of James Valdoe but she was aware that there were those who walked warily where he was concerned. In the end, putting her trust in her husband's judgement, she gave him a brief outline of Elaine's story.

'So you are looking for a husband for her against heavy odds. What sort of man have you in mind?'

Gertie spread her hands. 'A comfortable man, comfortably

circumstanced, willing and able to disregard her lack of fortune.'

He laughed. 'I understand now why you find my interest in Miss Marney so alarming. You see me as deficient in the first attribute and over-endowed in the second.'

'Well, no one would be so foolish as to call you a *comfortable* man,' Gertie returned. 'What Fanny and I both hope for Elaine is that she should find some happiness in marriage.'

'Which you do not see me providing. Have you someone in view for the girl?'

'Yes. No. I do not know. The man I hoped for has not come to town. A death in the family.'

'Most inconvenient. How does Miss Marney regard the matter?'

'She is, fortunately, blessed with uncommon good sense and prepared to apply it.'

'At nineteen? Remarkable! Do you not think that with the examples of your marriage and Fanny's before her she might entertain some hope for a share of romance?'

Before Gertie could reply to that Elaine returned and the question was left unanswered.

When Braxted and Elaine had gone, Gertie thought over what had been said and realized that James had revealed nothing of his feelings. He had been fencing with her and more than ever, she found herself wishing Sheffney had not allowed himself to be inveigled into undertaking the diplomatic mission that had already kept them apart longer than expected by either of them. What she needed most at this time was the benefit of his better knowledge of the Marquis of Braxted. . . .

Braxted's choice of vehicle was a curricle. Its colour was a rich crimson, dark almost to black, with the wheels and thin trimline picked out in buff and the same colour used for the upholstery.

83

His tiger, who would sit behind them as a necessary balance for the two-wheeled vehicle, was in livery to match, his striped waist-coat proclaiming his office. He stood to the heads of a pair of dun-coloured horses, that were as near to buff in colour as possible.

When they reached the park Elaine was made aware of the difference between Miss Marney being seen in the company of a little-known gentleman such as Mr Raffen, and being seen sitting up beside the Marquis of Braxted. It seemed to her that half of those taking air, whether walking or riding, wished to have a few words with His Lordship in order to stare their fill at his companion.

Glimpsing the quirk of Elaine's eyebrows after being released from a haughty matron's lengthy inspection, Braxted said amusedly, 'Being stared at is consequent on complying with society's demand that one should be seen in the right place at the right time.'

'And with the right person?' Elaine quipped lightly.

He gave her a gleaming look and an acknowledging nod. 'Eschewing false modesty, I can only say, yes, Miss Marney – with the right person.'

'Then I must thank you, my lord, for your favour.'

'That, I think, is tantamount to a set-down.'

'Not at all. I wish only to acknowledge your kindness.'

'Kindness is not one of my virtues. I am reasonably just, I hope, but I am not kind.'

Elaine threw him a quizzical look but did not speak.

Braxted smiled and was about to speak again when a slim, dark-haired gentleman riding by with two officers in Rifleman Green caught his eye and gave him a cheery wave. Braxted bowed and half turned to gaze after the three riders for a moment. Almost to himself, he said as he turned back, 'Poor Slender Billy! He's a shade too modest for the age. As Princess

Charlotte's fiancé he deserves better than to have to lodge with his tailor.'

'They say the Princess is not happy with the match. Will she be kept to it?' Elaine wondered aloud.

Braxted returned his attention to her. 'Castlereagh has persuaded the Regent of the desirability of the union and His Highness, having decreed it, does not care to have his will opposed.' His tone was dry.

'I have heard the Prince of Orange spoken of as a very amiable young man, but if Princess Charlotte has taken him in dislike will her father compel her to marry him? And how will she bear it if he does?'

'Fathers have dictated – or attempted to dictate – whom their sons and daughters should marry since time began. Princes usually have the best excuse for the practice.' This was said in an even drier tone. 'But you are unlikely to have such a dictate forced on you. Your parents died while you were still a child, I understand.'

'Yes.'

'Losing their loving kindness must have been grievous to you.'

'The loss of my mother's was, yes. Loving kindness was not a notable characteristic in my father,' she said with a rueful twinkle.

'He was unkind?'

'Oh no. It was just that there was no *warmth* in his nature. He was a scholarly man. My ability to learn won his approbation, but if he loved me for myself I cannot remember that he ever showed it.' Voice and expression softening, she went on, 'Losing my mother, however, was dreadful to me. My mirror tells me I resemble her in looks and that gives me some sort of comfort. I wish I could claim my disposition was like hers, but I have nothing of her gentleness, her sweetness. And certainly I could never be as patiently submissive to anyone as she was to my father.'

85

'Perhaps the pliancy of her nature made her happy to depend on his authority.'

'Perhaps,' Elaine agreed, but there was no agreement in her tone. A little hurriedly, she turned back to the royal family. 'The Prince Regent's own marriage is not a happy one. His open animosity to his wife is what alienates many people.'

'And supports Princess Charlotte's plea for her betrothal to be dissolved, could he but see it. His marriage was the price exacted by his father for being again heavily in debt and was doomed before ever it was solemnized. Princess Caroline is the daughter of His Majesty's favourite sister and the king presented her to the Prince as his only choice. It was a marriage of total incompatibility. The Prince is fastidious in his person and the lady proved to be less so. To that she added the manners of a hoyden – the antithesis of his. No doubt the lady was wronged, too, but that aside, when he left her, the citizenry, as perverse as they so often are, espoused the lady's cause without the least understanding of what lies between the two.'

'But the cartoons in the papers depict the Regent as so gross . . . as such a monster of degeneracy. One cannot help but wonder how much truth—' Too late, Elaine remembered she was speaking to a man reputed to be a close friend of the Regent. Blushing vividly, she said, 'I beg your pardon. I should not have said— I had forgotten—'

He brushed her words aside. 'His faults are those of the times and no worse than most other men's, except perhaps in the matter of extravagance for which his people have to pay and naturally resent. Even that has some excuse in being an extreme reaction to his father's parsimony. He is a talented man whose talents have never been allowed a proper expression. The repression he suffered under was heavy-handed but inevitable issuing as it did from what our late waspish observer, Horace Walpole, named "the palace of piety". Small wonder then, that an intelligent, spirited young man ran riot when he could. As for his much-advertised *amours* – I do not see them as so much worse than those indulged in by half the husbands in England.'

'That must be the saddest comment on marriage of all, sir.'

For a moment or two his cool dark gaze quizzed her. Then he said, 'How serious we are! Should we not be discussing bonnets and balls, parties and plays?'

'If you prefer such subjects, we will. I believe cocquelot is the colour with which we are all to trim our bonnets and gowns this year. What do you—?'

'Do not dare, Miss Marney! I would rather discuss the new electro-chemical theory the Swedes are about to launch on the world. Instead, I will continue my defence of the Regent in the hope that there may be one other who will judge him with understanding. I don't doubt you have heard the charge laid at the Prince's door that he failed to keep his promise to his friend, Mr Fox, to bring the Whigs into government when he had the power. The Whigs continue to make enough noise about it! But Fox had been five years dead and the Whigs had fallen apart before that power fell to the Prince. Wellington, meanwhile, had had his great victories and the Regent understood their significance. If he had kept the promise he made Fox, we should not now be celebrating Napoleon's downfall because the Whigs refused to abate their intention to abandon Wellington, to recall the army and leave Europe to its fate. I tell you, Miss Marney, that the Prince was as much the architect of the victory we are currently celebrating as were Wellington, Blücher and the rest.'

'For a man who disowns kindness,' Elaine said smilingly, 'it seems to me you have a considerable kindness for His Royal Highness.'

'As I have said, it is more a sense of justice. There are many, however, who could testify to the *Prince's* kindness if they chose, or he permitted it.'

What more might have been said was cut off by both in the same moment having their attention drawn to an approaching phaeton. Neat, unexceptional, in the purist's choice of dark olive green and drawn by a well-matched pair of light bays. Elaine at once recognized it and its occupants: Mr Cato Raffen and Miss Georgina Pilford, the Dendleby heiress. They looked, she thought dourly, well satisfied with each other's company being deep in animated and laughing conversation.

Quite unconsciously, her lip curled. Mr Raffen appeared to be doing what Gertie had wished and was improving his acquaintance with the wealthy young lady. She, for her part, was doing nothing to discourage him. As pretty in sunlight as she had looked in candlelight, her bonnet was a mere effervescence of stiffened lace and forget-me-nots and her gauzy white gown was trimmed to match. Engrossed with Miss Pilford, the two vehicles were level before Cato showed awareness of who it was they were passing. He saw Braxted first and it was only after they had exchanged bows that his gaze travelled on to meet Elaine's. He bowed again, but with a mischievous lift of his brows that might have been a response to her forbidding expression or a comment on the eminence of her companion – or possibly both.

Braxted caught the look and said as the two vehicles passed, 'It was Gertie who made you acquainted with Mr Raffen, I imagine. How do you like the gentleman?'

She did not correct his error but merely answered his question. 'My acquaintance with him is slight so I have not yet formed a reliable opinion.' It was stiff and not what she believed.

Braxted said no more regarding Mr Raffen and soon after, their slow circuit of the park being complete, he headed the curricle back to Sheffney House.

Gertie could see nothing in the manner of either to increase her anxiety when the two returned. Braxted, urbane and unrevealing as ever, remained only long enough to say a graceful goodbye and Elaine saw him go with her usual composure.

With a small sigh of relief, Her Ladyship asked, 'Did you enjoy the drive? I expect you encountered a good many stares.'

'We did, but after a while I managed to ignore them.'

Elaine had taken off her bonnet and was shaking out her curls. She had spoken with such unconcern, Gertie wondered if the girl had any understanding of the magnitude of her apparent conquest. Probing a little deeper, she asked, 'And what do you think of the marquis on closer acquaintance?'

Elaine gave brief thought to her answer. 'Though he is very easy to talk to, all that I learned of him today was that he has a genuine kindness for the Prince Regent. All in all, I think I quite like him.' She smiled sunnily at Gertie and went upstairs to tidy herself.

All in all, I think I quite like him! Lightly and coolly said. Gertie's own smile was touched with malice. How she wished that the noble marquis had heard the schoolmaster's daughter's qualified valuation of him. He was not a vain man; even so, it must surely have done him good.

CHAPTER EIGHT

a few days later, close on the dinner-hour of eight o'clock, Elaine walked into the small and pretty room known as the Primrose Parlour looking for Gertie. The room's occupant, however, was not the one she sought. Sprawled in one of the comfortable chairs was Cato Raffen, as deeply unconscious as any of the Seven Sleepers.

His failure to come to Sheffney House during the past several weeks had strengthened rather than softened Elaine's unfriendly feelings towards him. So disobliging was the man he could not even give her the opportunity to allow him to see her disgust of him. Asleep, he was still out of reach and she turned away with increased irritation, but found herself drawn back to look at him again. What had he been doing to exhaust himself to the point of falling asleep in someone else's house? He was not dressed for visiting but for riding, with every evidence about him of hard travel. Where had he been? What doing?

It was a small amend to her vanity to have him for once at a disadvantage and be able to study him at her leisure without meeting the unnerving penetration of his grey gaze. Under the thick, dark, richly brown hair, his face was one of straight lines, the bones subtly drawn under the brown skin, his mouth, even in sleep, hinting at the steely, smiling determination of the man. It did not look the face of a cheat – but wasn't it part of every Machiavellian rogue to look honest?

A scar not noticed before caught her attention and she bent lower to trace the hair-thin line which stretched from an inch in front of his left ear to below his jaw. Another memento of a desperate adventure?

His uncomplaining, laughing account of how his left hand had been damaged came into her mind and she realized how little thought she had given to the hazards he must face in what had been – and might still be – an adventurous way of life. A way that Gertie had hinted had been thrust on him rather than chosen. 'As unfortunate in his family as you in yours' Gertie had said. His perfidy forgotten for the moment, Elaine's expression softened as her study of him intensified.

Possibly, it was that intensity which drew Raffen up from the black pit of sleep into which he had fallen. He was not fully awake when her face came hazily into focus. Her shadowed eyes and softly curving lips gave her expression a musing tenderness. Still in a half-dream, he reached up to bring her head down until her lips met his and he could take all the sweet generosity they appeared to be offering.

For a moment she was too astonished to move and her mouth remained yielding and gentle. But when his kiss began to deepen, to ask more, her recoil brought him abruptly to full consciousness and he released her.

She was gazing at him as though in disbelief, a hand clasped to her mouth.

Guilt and vexation assailed him together. Rising hurriedly, he captured the hand hanging at her side and said lightly, 'You see how dangerous it is to invade a man's dreams. But it was a kiss given in innocence, I swear!'

It had begun so, he thought, but he could not swear to it having continued so. Nor did Miss Marney's expression offer much hope of her belief in his innocence.

He smiled coaxingly at her. 'Miss Marney I cannot apologize for something that, to me, was entirely pleasurable, but I swear I was more than half asleep.'

'I make no claim to having enjoyed a similar pleasure, Mr Raffen,' Elaine said with a primness and severity all the greater for not being entirely truthful. At first there had been only surprise, but then, she knew, for a moment or two there had been a wondering felicity in the experience – swiftly ended when her mind had leapt to the alert. She tried now to tug her hand from his grip and when she could not, frowned and said crossly, 'Be good enough to let me go, sir.'

He complied. Asked contritely, 'Must we be at outs again?'

'Again? When have we *not* been? It hardly needed what has just occurred to confirm me in my opinion that guile comes naturally to you, Mr Raffen.'

That puzzled him. He had thought that following their drive in Hyde Park they had parted in accord with one another and since then he had seen her only to bow to in Hyde Park. He regarded her now with rueful exasperation. She did not have the sophistication to pass the incident over as unimportant, which, in his view, it was. Indeed, he had met fifteen year olds with more worldly wisdom than this prickly young woman, but he knew that was being unfair to her when he recalled the circumstances in which he had first seen her.

Looking at her, with a flush on her cheeks and green fire in her eyes, there was nothing he wanted so much at this minute as to kiss her again, and then again, deeply, satisfyingly . . . to feel her melt, yield. . . . It was a pity, he reflected, that it did not occur to her that if he were the villain she thought him he would very likely have done just that. Nor did Miss Marney seem to know anything of her disturbing ability to loose the old serpent in a man.

He was still seeking some way of mollifying her when the door opened and Gertie came to his rescue.

'Cato! How glad I am to see you again!' she said, holding out both hands to him. 'Where have you been? What have you been doing these past weeks? I demand to be told!'

Elaine found the memory of Cato Raffen's kiss lingered uncomfortably with her. A first experience but uninvited and therefore to be remembered with indignation, so she told herself. He had claimed to be half asleep . . . dreaming. How many women did he kiss in his dreams? She reminded herself of the perfidious wink she had seen in the mirror when they had returned from their drive in Hyde Park. Even for that, she suspected, if asked, Mr Raffen would find some easy excuse . . . would *smile, and smile, and be a villain. . . .*

He had declined to remain for dinner, had told them little of what he had been doing beyond admitting with a shrug and a laugh that he had covered a lot of ground in a short time and yes, it had to do with the Marquis of Braxted and the Prince Regent and, yes, it was possible there was a plot against the Regent's life, but it was all very shadowy and might yet come to nothing. Meanwhile, he was sure he could rely on their discretion not to speak of it to anyone else. Rumours easily got out of hand.

Elaine had slept poorly that night. There had been dreams, but she could recall nothing of them except that they left an uneasiness that remained with her even after she awoke.

She breakfasted alone, Gertie, as she often did, taking hers in bed and rising a leisurely hour or two later. As she left the dining-room, she was approached by one of the maids.

'Miss. . . .' The girl felt in the pocket of her apron and brought out a piece of paper. 'I found this in the Primrose Parlour under the blue chair. I can't make out what it says but it doesn't look much.'

The paper was creased as though it had been crumpled in someone's hand but being thick and coarse, it had sprung open again. In a laboured, uneducated hand, she read:

he nows how you are dont go to hide park satrday.

She puzzled over it for a moment until her mind suggested a rearrangement that made sense. *He knows who you are. . . .* A clear warning, intended for Cato Raffen who yesterday had sat in the blue chair. A warning linked to his 'covering a lot of ground' and a plot that was not so shadowy as he had tried to make them think?

She stared down at the note as if it could tell her more than it did. Then remembering the maid, she looked up and said, 'Thank you. You did right to give me this.'

The maid bobbed a curtsy and went on her way. Elaine remained where she was, her mind busy. The note, having been read, had been roughly crumpled in either contempt or anger, she guessed. But then, overtaken by his desperate need for sleep, it had probably fallen from Raffen's hand to be blown under the chair by a draught from the door when it was opened. And though the note might have been forgotten, he would not have forgotten its contents, she was sure. She was equally sure that far from being a deterrent, the warning would ensure that Raffen went to Hyde Park. And today was Saturday!

Swept on a tide of urgency, she was halfway up the stairs to her room to fetch bonnet and shawl before she was aware of having made a decision. She was going to the park, but *why* – or what she hoped to achieve – she did not know. She accepted her decision and closed her mind to all else. She told no one what she intended and luck, so she thought it, being with her, she passed out of the house, unseen and unhindered.

The streets between Berkeley Square and Hyde Park were as

quiet as she had expected; a carriage or two, a woman crying cresses, a baker's dog-drawn cart, which was no more than a box on wheels with the baker's boy trotting beside it. The day was fine but she found herself walking against a gusty wind and for all her hurry, somewhere a clock was striking ten as she entered the park.

Despite the departure of so many notables and early as it was, there were still many people about, for there were still sights to be seen. General Blücher might be glimpsed riding by, or one or more of the handful of Cossacks still remaining. These were famous not only for the strangeness of their dress, but their practice of drinking oil out of street lamps, so plunging whole areas of London into darkness, and for appropriating to themselves, good-humouredly and without disguise, any unattended article that took their fancy – behaviour that was looked on with remarkable tolerance.

Nothing more remarkable by way of entertainment seemed to be expected. Whether walking or riding, everyone was proceeding at a leisurely pace and now, at last, she was brought to pause and forced to ask herself what in the name of sanity she was doing here? No time of day had been mentioned in the warning note. If by sheer chance she located Cato Raffen in the expanse of parkland around her, what did she intend to do? What did it matter to her if he chose to throw himself in the way of danger? What stupid impulse had brought her here when she had a positive dislike of the man? There was only one sensible option open to her and that was to return to Sheffney House as quickly as she could and hope to re-enter the house as easily as she had left it.

She turned back on her path and found it blocked by a man who had been approaching her from behind. With a wide, ingratiating smile, he said, 'Need a man's arm to help you keep your feet against this wind, miss?'

She glared at him for a long moment before finding her voice.

'No, indeed. My friends are waiting for me,' she told him forbiddingly and swinging to her left, set off across an expanse of grass as though intending to join a gossiping group gathered not too far away.

Once sure the man had passed out of sight, she turned aside again on to a path sheltered by bushes. There, she paused to straighten her wind-buffeted bonnet and fold her silk shawl more closely about her. And it was then that she became aware she was no longer hearing just the voice of the wind itself. In rough bursts, there came to her the sound of a number of voices, distant but growing louder and raised in a cacophony of hate such as she had heard more than once raised against the unfortunate Regent.

Could the Regent be here today after all? Or had the mob found some other unfortunate object on which to vent their snarling disfavour? Elaine stood irresolute, torn between a reawakened urge to go forward and simple common sense that beseeched her return to Sheffney House.

Others were responding to the lure of excitement however, and before she had made up her mind, she was caught in a sudden rush of people from behind and carried with them towards the clamour.

Hemmed in, hurried on, the rapidly growing crowd's excitement was hot and pulsing. If anything was wanting to impress her with her own stupidity, it was her inability to escape. Behind her, three young men had linked arms in order to maintain their leading place and, incidently, hers. It was not only impossible for her to turn but would have put her in danger of falling beneath the feet of the rest. Speech in such circumstances was worse than useless.

When what appeared to be an impenetrable wall of people lining the rails of the perimeter carriage route could be seen, the throng veered away in search of a clear space and one being found, veered back bringing Elaine with bruising force up against the waist high top rail of the fence.

The centre of the crowd's attention was off to her right and concentrated on the line of vehicles coming slowly towards where she stood. Stones and every other possible missile were being hurled at the leading carriage which, together with the howling, shrieking concerto of hate, accounted for the slowness of the approach as the frightened horses reared and fought against their bits.

When the leading carriage drew level with Elaine, the insignia of the Prince Regent was just visible through the dust and abrasions disfiguring its sides. That someone occupied the carriage she was able to see but not plainly enough to recognize.

The voice of the mob rolled onward with the carriage which by now was nearing an exit from the park. The excitement of those around her began to abate and gave Elaine hope of being able to extricate herself from among them before long. But suddenly new waves of movement began to pass through the packed mass of bodies and she found herself again being thrust with dangerous force against the rail. The din too, was rolling back on itself with a new note in it – a note of alarm. Her own movements were too restricted by pressure to allow her to do more than cling to the rail for support and pray for release as the passing procession of carriages thinned.

She was gazing helplessly across the carriageway when she saw Cato Raffen. He was blocked in as she was and appeared to be trying to force a way out. Though the crowd was less dense on that side, there too, it was moved by surges that were generated by some power outside itself. Briefly, a little space appeared around Raffen as though someone had fallen. Into that space an arm was extended, the hand holding a pistol and the pistol was levelled at Raffen.

She did not know whether she screamed his name aloud, or whether it was no more than an intention. There was little chance of a shot or individual voice being heard above the continuing tumult. All Elaine knew was that Raffen's head turned, his body twisted and he vanished from view. She was given no chance to see more. The crowd around her turned as a tide turns, backing against itself, powered now by panic. Elaine was carried with it, as helpless as before, mere flotsam on the flood.

It was worse than before. Wedged between bodies in rough, odorous clothes, pierced through by the screams of others caught up and as powerless as herself, she fought to keep upright, fought against the terror of falling and being trampled underfoot. Her arms were pinned to her sides and, as air was relentlessly squeezed from her lungs, she knew her senses were darkening.

She was close to suffocation, when a heavy impact lifted her off her feet as a man drove his way with brutal determination across the forward surge carrying her with him. Darkness engulfed her.

She knew nothing then until she found herself dragging painful gasps of air into her starved lungs. Slowly her senses cleared and she discovered that somehow she had been propelled out of the crush and was now jammed against the rough trunk of a tree, held against it and shielded by the lean length of a man's body while he clung with savage determination to the lowest branches.

After-shocks of the blows and collisions from which her rescuer was protecting her came through to her for a while, then those, too, ended and the ground shook instead to the passing of a small detachment of mounted soldiers. Only when the man released his grip on the tree was she able to look up and recognize Lieutenant Dacier.

Weak and shaking, she almost fell when he stepped back from her and at once his arm went round her in support. The danger had been too extreme for embarrassment and Elaine's aching lungs supplied only enough air for her to whisper in a voice scarcely recognizable as her own, 'Thank you. Oh, thank you!'

Unbelievably, there was a clear hint of gaiety in the tone of his disclaimer. '*La bonne chance!* I make the *pousser*, the push, for me, my sake – and there you are!' He shook his head at her. 'But how does it happen? For you to be alone among the *canaille*?'

The brown eyes smiling down at her were alight with excitement and she realized that he had actually relished the danger, the fight to survive. But he had been a soldier and surviving a battle must always be a reason for triumph, she supposed.

She did not answer his question, merely shook her head and hoped he thought her too shocked to have gathered her wits yet. He was shrugging off his buttonless jacket now and a moment later had draped it about her shoulders. Only then did she realize that not only had she lost her bonnet and shawl, but her torn gown revealed an immodest amount of her shift and herself.

The easy, tactful manner in which Dacier performed the service did not allow for more than a moment's embarrassment and with similar quiet efficiency and the offer of a gold coin, he enticed one the several urchins already searching among the scattered debris for articles of value, to find a hackney and bring it to the nearest gate.

'It is not far. Can you walk?' he asked.

'Yes,' she said without knowing if it were true. But as they moved out on to the path, she saw other victims of the mob's frenzy in worse case than herself. Dacier would not allow her to stop. She was in no state to give help, and there were others there already doing what they could.

The good sense of his decree soon became apparent. The short distance to the gate where the hackney was waiting took most of what little strength had returned to her limbs and she was incapable of climbing into the vehicle. With no more ado, the lieutenant lifted her into the vehicle and held her until she was safely seated before climbing in himself.

It was as she relaxed back against the squabs that the memory of what had taken her to the park and what she had witnessed there flooded in on her. She closed her eyes but could not prevent tears from sliding down her cheeks, but whether she wept from shock, or fear, or sorrow she did not know. Dacier was regarding her anxiously and taking one of her hands in his, held it for a brief moment in a warm clasp. 'Poor young lady! It was an experience most disagreeable, was it not?'

She gulped back her tears and tried again to thank him, but as before, he swept her words aside and began to talk lightly of a pleasant walk to a friend's house turning into an affair of the most unexpected when he had been *engoulé* – swallowed up – by the mob as she had.

Afraid he might again ask her what she was doing in the park alone, she asked hastily, 'Do you know how it all began?'

Dacier gave a twisted smile and shrugged. 'Your Prince Regent . . . he drive in the park. The people do not like. They run to *siffler* – to hiss, make noise, throw the *gravier*. First the carriage drives fast but others are in the way and it must slow and the horses make trouble. The people grow more angry. They wish *démontrer* . . . to show. . . . It is as you say, a pretty to-do. Presently, the soldiers ride into the crowd and the people run. All is confusion.'

The hackney drew up outside Sheffney House and it occurred to Elaine that she still had an ordeal to face. How was she to explain her actions to Gertie?

But Gertie, on the point of sending both the footmen and a groom out to search for Elaine, or at least for news of her, looked at the girl's white, stricken face, her ruined dress. and postponed asking for explanations. A shawl was produced to cover her disarray and she was handed into Polly Cutts's care to be taken to her room and ministered to. Before she went, Dacier again took one of her hands in his. This time to raise it to his lips in a warm salute.

Resuming his jacket, he stayed only long enough to tell Gertie as much of the story as he knew, then, once more declining to be thanked for his part in it, he left.

Gertie, speculating with some misgiving on what had taken Elaine to Hyde Park, wondered if she had gone to keep an assignation. Until today the girl's behaviour had been exemplary, but what else could have induced her to slip out of the house so secretly and go unaccompanied to a place open to all and sundry? Had she fallen love? With someone quite unsuitable? Or – heaven forbid! – had she gone to meet Jeremy?

She closed her eyes at the thought of the trouble that could create in her brother-in-law's family. . . .

CHAPTER NINE

*H*aving drunk the wine Polly handed her, Elaine lay on her bed her mind awash with problems and harsh fears and with no expectation of sleeping. But sleep she did because, unknown to her – and daringly for a rather stolid young woman – Polly had laced the wine with one or two drops of laudanum. She woke two hours later feeling more in command of herself though the stiffness and bruising of her body were more painfully noticeable and all her worries lay in wait.

While she washed her face and hands and dressed in a clean gown, she tried to think of how she could explain to Gertie what had impelled her to go to Hyde Park. How could she confess the foolish truth when she was so far from understanding it herself? And darkly clouding and confusing her thoughts was her dread of what had, or might have, happened to Cato Raffen. Apart from all else, if she told Gertie what she had seen, it would be to pass on to Gertie the fear and grief of not knowing the outcome.

But how could she give any explanation at all if she left out all mention of Cato Raffen? The most she would be able to offer was that she had gone to the park on a whim and suffer being thought both stupid and thoughtless. She deserved it. Her action had been worse than that, she acknowledged to herself: it had been irrational. What could she have possibly have hoped to achieve? And *why* should she concern herself in Mr Raffen's affairs?

It was in a very unhappy mood that she went downstairs.

To open the door to the Primrose Parlour and see Cato Raffen standing in the middle of the room, apparently quite unharmed, held her dazed and unbelieving on the threshold. Gertie must have been telling him about the morning's events for he swung round to face the door instantly, a dark scowl already in place on his face. Ignoring any kind of greeting, he said, 'Well, Miss Marney, what have you been about? Doing your best, so I hear, to be trampled to death by the rabble!'

His tone suggested she had engaged in an activity designed especially to provoke him. Out of a tangle of feelings, anger surfaced. She gave him a long, glacial look and an ironically deep curtsy to point his discourtesy and vex him further. Straightening, she said, 'How very pleasant to see you again so soon, Mr Raffen.'

His mouth tightened ominously. Gertie, looking from one to the other, said with some asperity, 'Now that you have greeted each other so delightfully perhaps you will both be seated.' The antipathy between these two was incomprehensible to her. And tiresome. Easy and pleasant as each was when apart, brought together they were flint and tinder. To Elaine, as she seated herself, she said, 'By coincidence, Cato was also in Hyde Park this morning, but unlike you, he managed not to be borne away by the crowd.'

There was no hint in her tone that anything more than coincidence had brought about their dual presence, Elaine noticed thankfully, as Gertie turned back to Cato to say, 'You were telling me something about Carlton House when I interrupted to tell you of Elaine's misadventure. . . . '

'Not Carlton House precisely, but His Highness's stables. As you can imagine, there was considerable lament over the damage

104

the Regent's carriage had suffered from the stones and whatever else had been hurled at it. A rather graver cause for concern was the discovery of what appears to be a bullet-hole in one of the windows. The bullet – and having seen the hole there is little doubt in my mind that such it was – had not passed straight through or the opposite window would have shattered. A thorough search of the carriage was still being made when I left. No one has reported hearing a shot, but the hullabaloo in the park was so great it would have covered even the discharge of a pistol.'

'What caused the rumpus? Set the mob going?'

'Public feeling against him has been growing again since it slipped out that Princess Charlotte wants to be free of the Prince of Orange, particularly as marriage to him would entail her living outside this country. The popular belief is that her father would be glad for her to go, in the same way as he would be delighted to see the back of her mother.' He paused frowning, and said thoughtfully, 'What is curious is that the Prince's decision to take an early, quiet and unremarked drive in the park was only made in the evening of yesterday. The crowd's presence was nothing out of the ordinary, but whoever waited for him with a gun, knew the Prince would be there.'

'As *you* did! How did you?' Gertie regarded him with bright, inquisitive eyes.

He returned her a wolfish smile. 'I will tell you all in good time, Gertie, but I cannot tell everything yet. Even what I have told you today must not be passed on, though it may well leak out before long. I saw Braxted on my way here and he expects the matter will be suppressed if possible, if only to prevent ideas being put into other minds.'

'From what you say, I collect this has to do with what James has involved you in?'

'So it appears.'

105

'Then there definitely *is* a plot against the Regent's life! Are you on the way to learning who is behind it?'

'Little more than a direction in which to look. His Highness's determined chivalry towards a certain lady made for a slow start.'

He caught Gertie's expression and laughed. 'Yes, of course, there had to be a lady in the affair, but, no, Gertie my dear, I do not intend to reveal her name. She it was who passed the warning to the Prince though the first alarm was sounded by an underling who put his own life at risk in doing so.' And, incidentally, mine for discovering it, he thought ruefully, remembering the murderous attack in the lane at Ringlestones He had suspected even then that the seaman had not been the Prince's would-be assassin but had been acting on his own behalf; now he was sure of it.

Elaine saw the grim little smile that accompanied the thought and wondered if he had known that a gun had been levelled at *him* that morning.

Cato was on his feet again. 'Well, find the assassin, I must, both for the Prince's sake and to satisfy myself. His Highness makes it all too easy for a killer to get close to him. Even now, Braxted tells me, he has declared he will not be separated from his people, either by secluding himself, or by surrounding himself with a ring of soldiers. *Noblesse oblige* is fine and dandy, but not when one's life is at stake. Someone has to save him from his foolhardiness. *As was necessary in another case!*' He shot a look at Elaine, but gave her no chance to respond. 'Now, for heaven's sake, let us speak of other things. Do you mean to go to this Relford affair? If you do, may I have the pleasure of escorting you? The Prince has matters that will keep him securely within doors that day, so I am informed.'

Yes, their intention was to go, Gertie told him, and accepting the offer of his escort, added with careful lack of emphasis, 'We are to take Miss Pilford with us.'

He gave her a glinting smile, and said smoothly, 'An added felicity. At what hour shall I present myself?'

The necessary details settled, he was ready to go. Now, looking at Elaine, he noticed what he had overlooked before when anger at the unnecessary danger she had been in had blurred his vision. She was very pale, a bruise was beginning to show colour above the scooped neckline of her dress and there was a long scratch on her right forearm. He knew the power of the mob. She would have other and worse bruises beneath her clothes. He remembered the churlish way he had greeted her. Every encounter with Miss Marney seemed tangled in error and frustration. What did he want from her? It was clear enough that she wanted nothing from him. . . .

He bowed towards her, said formally, 'I trust you will soon recover from any ill effects of your unfortunate adventure, Miss Marney.'

As formally, she replied, 'I am obliged to you, sir.'

He had meant what he said: she had not. With that to prick him, he left.

There could be no further delay to the explanation and apology Elaine owed Gertie – and how lame both sounded in her own ears! A stupid impulse . . . the early hour . . . few people in the park . . . no special reason. . . . Impossible to avoid the small lies, unimportant though they were. Her apologies however, were genuine. But if anything further was wanted to convince her that the expedition to the park had been ridiculous, Cato Raffen's visit would have done it. Demonstrably, he was more than capable of looking after himself.

Though Gertie accepted both explanation and apology, Elaine suspected her belief in the her protégée's good sense must be severely shaken.

The subject was dropped then and Gertie turned back to the Relfords' ridotto. As she had said to Elaine when the invitation had first arrived, it was one those places that *had* to be visited. The house, Reedshefe, an enlarged medieval manor house, overlooking the river at Chiswick, was famous for its gardens. The grounds had been first laid out by Bridgeman who, it was said, had invented that useful deceit, the *ha-ha*. Embellishments had been added later by William Kent and the whole was now considered to have an idyllic disposal of borders, statuary, *salle de verdure*, water, and serpentine paths winding through groves and wilderness.

'It is deplorable that Mrs Scott-Wharton, having undertaken to sponsor Miss Pilford through the season, should make so little effort on the girl's behalf,' Gertie said. 'However, it is a good opportunity to bring her and Cato together again in charming surroundings. A match between them would be an excellent thing for Cato, providing him with the fortune he needs and the advantage to her would be in getting a better man than most as husband.'

With less confidence in Gertie's final assertion, Elaine asked a little sourly, 'Will Miss Pilford's family favour the match?'

'Oh, there can be no difficulty *there*. Miss Pilford's father is no more than a country gentleman with a small estate. Her fortune derives from her maternal grandfather who was in trade, but Cato, when his brother dies, will be Baron Meldreth. He might look higher for a bride.'

It was the first Elaine had heard of Cato Raffen being heir to a barony, a surprise in itself. But Gertie had phrased the information oddly. She said, 'You said *when* his brother dies, as though it is expected.'

'Well, it is. And I could wish it had happened long ago!'

Such malevolence from Gertie made Elaine blink in surprise.

Gertie nodded. 'Yes, I know! A savage and unchristian thing to say, but not said without reason.' She paused a moment then decided that Elaine might look on Cato with more tolerance if she knew a little more about him. She said, 'Cato's father was a man from the old days . . . a big, burly man who did nothing in moderation. A roistering fool who drank too much, gambled too much and paid small heed to his responsibilities. His elder son, Julian, was a close copy of himself and prized for being so. Cato, his second son, being of a different cast entirely, was despised by both. I met him in an odd sort of way a little before my sixteenth birthday when I was sent to my godmother in Burghclere in Wiltshire in the hope that a change of air would speed my recovery from a bout of fever. The Meldreth estate, Eldenshaw, is not far from Burghclere. One day, walking to the village across a meadow with one of my godmother's maids, we came on a small boy sobbing his heart out over a puppy with a broken leg. His brother had lashed out with his booted foot at the animal over some misdemeanour and then run off. By good luck, the maid had been born and bred in Burghclere and knew of an old farrier with a reputation as a bone-setter and I persuaded her we should all go at once to ask his help.'

She crinkled a wry look at Elaine. 'The pup's leg was set and I asked his small owner to call and let me know how he went on. You may think it odd for a friendship to form between a sixteen-year-old girl and a boy of eight, but it did and because I visited my godmother as often as I could, being sure of being outrageously spoiled, the friendship had opportunity to continue through the years, even after I married.'

She frowned then, as less pleasant memories crowded in. 'When Cato was twenty his father and brother, following a long drinking session, drove out to visit a kindred spirit. Crossing a narrow bridge over the Enborne at reckless speed, the light whiskey Julian was driving overturned. His father was thrown into the river and being knocked unconscious, drowned before help arrived. Julian fell on his back across the stone wall of the bridge and has been paralysed from the waist down ever since.

Slowly, the paralysis is creeping upward. One day, as he has long known, it will kill him. Being the kind of man he is, he confronts his fate with fury, most of which is directed towards the brother who will inherit. In sheer malevolence of spirit, he is doing all he can to destroy Eldenshaw and waste what remains of the family fortune not already gambled away by him and his father. Beside the title, all Cato can hope to inherit is a hopelessly encumbered estate. Such is the degree of Julian's unreasonable spite, that his first act when he became Lord Meldreth and was sufficiently recovered from his accident, was to cut off all funds to his brother. That was when Cato came to London and, through me, sought Sheffney's help in finding employment. Sheffney found him a post with the East India Company, which led to Cato's going to India. Sheffney has said that he was also of great use to the government while there.'

Gertie shook her head deprecatingly. 'It isn't a pretty story, and even now, chained to chair and bed as Julian is, he continues to live as wildly as his physical restrictions allow. Cato visited him recently in the hope that time might have had some softening influence. But nothing of the kind! Beginning with dislike, as his end approaches, what Julian now feels towards his brother appears to be sheer hatred. His dissipations have made him sicker in mind and body than he need be and the sight of Cato in sound health drives him into frenzy.'

It was an appalling story, Elaine thought. Impossible to hear without feeling sympathy for the one whose interests were so unjustifiably injured. She set it aside to mull over at some later time.

The day of the Relfords' ridotto proved kind, with warm sunshine, a light breeze to temper it and no more than the smallest of clouds sailing a summer-blue sky. On such a day, the open barouche, accommodating four people, was the natural choice of conveyance.

They called for Miss Pilford at her aunt's house in Mount Street and with commendable promptness the young lady appeared to take the vacant seat beside Gertie and opposite Cato Raffen, to smile prettily at them all and behave as charmingly as ever. Her addition to the party was both a relief and an irritation to Elaine; a relief because her presence laid claim to a share of Mr Raffen's attention, giving Elaine time in which to attempt to reconcile her annoyance with him and the sympathy Gertie's story had aroused. Her irritation sprang from how easily Miss Pilford drew not just a share, but almost the whole of that gentleman's attention. In a gown of cream-coloured Indian mull under a fragile tunic of pink spotted lustrine and with a shallow, pink-ribboned straw hat perched on her black curls she made as delightful a picture as any young woman possibly could.

Elaine had met her on one or two earlier occasions but too briefly to decide how much or how little she liked her. Rich, charming, pretty, the fact that her wealth was derived from trade could only be a small counterbalance to the rest. Given the size of her fortune and her good looks, she might even aspire to being a countess Gertie had said on one occasion. Would she – as Gertie hoped – be content with a mere baron?

Country dancing on the lawns had already begun when they arrived at Reedshefe and there were gentlemen enough eager to offer themselves as partners to the younger ladies and afterwards act as guides to the special features of the gardens.

Cato danced once with each of the girls but gave place with good grace to others, content, it appeared, to remain with Gertie and watch the company with the faintly humorous expression that seemed never to be absent from his eyes for long. There was a brief occasion when no one had come to claim Elaine's company and he considered asking her to dance with him again. She was looking towards him at that moment and perhaps she read the intention in his face. She turned away with a swiftness

111

that seemed an intentional repulse, but before he could decide whether or not to tease her by making the application anyway they were joined by Jeremy Lazelle.

He was a late arrival and his mood was verging on petulant. The exchange of courtesies was brief and then with a challenging glance at his aunt-in-law, he claimed Elaine's company for a visit to the water garden. Gertie frowned at him but made no demur.

Observing the smiling willingness with which Miss Marney went with Lazelle, Cato felt irritation rise in him again at the distinction she seemed to draw between himself and other men. When Gertie was approached by three cronies clearly bent on an exchange of gossip, he was glad to be able to slip away and indulge his own disgruntled mood.

That Jeremy had a grievance was soon apparent to Elaine and in a rallying way she said presently, 'Well, I have done my best to promote a little conversation, but I perceive the water gardens may only be approached in solemn silence.'

Bursting from him as though the words could no longer be contained, Jeremy declared, 'I never see you these days!'

His vehemence startled Elaine. 'But that is because your guardsman duties have kept you more than usually busy, surely!'

'But not that alone! My aunt knew I was free today but she did not call on me to escort you here. Only when I called at Sheffney House did I discover you had come here. And *who* is Mr Raffen that he should be preferred as an escort?'

'A friend of Her Ladyship since childhood, so I understand. A kind of unofficial younger brother lately returned from a long stay in India,' she said soothingly.

'Invited for *your* benefit, I imagine.'

Elaine smiled. 'Well, no. For his own and Miss Pilford's. Like you, he is in need of a rich wife and she is a considerable heiress.'

He was not appeased. 'Then I suppose it is the Marquis of

Braxted she has in mind for you. He arrived an instant after me, though this is the kind of entertainment he *never* attends. Lately, the gentleman has done a number of things for which he is better noted for *not* doing, each time in *your* company. It is a matter of common gossip.'

Annoyed, Elaine told him, 'I have done less in the noble marquis's company than with many another and not for one moment have my thoughts turned to the expectation of a proposal from that quarter. Nor has he, I am certain, had any intention of making one. But it cannot signify to you what I have done or with whom – as you know!'

'But it does! It does! I cannot help myself!' Jeremy declared bitterly.

He had been hurrying her along at a far from leisurely rate and she had taken no note of their direction. She saw now that they had left the gardens and were approaching an area of woodland. Puzzled, she stopped.

'This cannot be the way to the water garden, surely?'

'No. But we must talk and we have no need of an audience.'

'I think we should not if it is to be in the same vein as what you have already said.'

He frowned down at her. 'You don't understand! I cannot go on with things as they are!'

There were voices behind them now and, glancing back, Elaine saw a group of laughing young people following the path they were on. Jeremy had taken a grip on her arm and she sensed that in his present, unusual mood he was not above making a scene.

'Very well,' she agreed reluctantly and walked on with him into the trees.

As soon as opportunity offered, Jeremy turned aside on to a lesser path and when they were well out of sight of the other walkers he drew her beneath the dark canopy of an ancient yew and transferred his grip to her shoulders. 'I cannot bear it,

113

Elaine,' he said fiercely. ' It seems that every man has the right to approach you except me.'

'But you know why. Our circumstances make it imposs—'

'The devil take our circumstances!' Jeremy growled, and pulling her into his arms, showered passionate kisses on her face and neck.

She struggled against him, but he was a strong young man who had had too long to work himself up into angry resentment against the comparative indigence that prevented him having what he wanted . . . perhaps had not wanted so badly until he thought he had at least one powerful rival. Never before in his twenty-three years had his capacity for self-denial been truly tested, and Elaine's apparent willingness to accept the prohibition they had been given struck at his youthful pride.

He smothered Elaine's protests with his mouth, while her struggles to push him away served only to increase his angry passion. Only when Elaine had managed to free an arm and delivered a hearty slap to his face was he jolted into releasing her. He stood staring at her then, in an acutely uncomfortable confusion of resentment, frustration and guilt.

Exasperated as she was, Elaine had, too, some feeling of guilt. If ever she had been on the way to being in love with Jeremy, she was not so now, she realized. Fond of him, yes, but not in love. Even hot, dishevelled and cross, she was not without sympathy for him.

Jeremy's breeding now came to his rescue. With stiff formality, he said, 'I apologize.'

'I'm sorry, too. That it should have come to this, I mean. But Jeremy, do think how uncomfortable you would find it to live in straitened circumstances . . . perhaps having to give up your horses. . . .'

The truth of that did nothing to soothe his temper. His return to good-manners came to an abrupt end. Gracelessly, he snarled,

114

'What I think is that you have a richer quarry in your sights now, and I can go the devil!'

'If that is your opinion, you will not be surprised to see me doing my best to attach His Lordship's affections.'

He was already conscious of the unworthiness of his last remark, but was driven to cap it. 'No, not in the least!'

'So now that we understand one another, will you please oblige me by going away.'

With awful civility, Jeremy said, 'I cannot leave you here alone. Allow me to escort you back to my aunt.'

'I think if you do not just go, I shall scream,' Elaine told him through her teeth.

Having dug the pit in which he found himself, the fact that Elaine did not intend to help him out of it made Jeremy feel sufficiently ill-used to respond resentfully, 'Very well,' and walk away from her.

Guilt pursued him, but injured feelings kept him going. If Elaine had cast herself in his arms, he told himself, had bemoaned the sadness of their situation, had wept even though she urged him to reaffirm his promise of renunciation, he would have felt differently, acted differently, knowing he did not suffer alone. *Then* he could have thought with tender melancholy of what might have been; could have accepted that another man, better placed than he, might win her. As it was—

As it was, he walked back towards the lawns brooding deeply, unaware of being already on the way to recovery from his first attack of lovesickness.

CHAPTER TEN

*T*ight-lipped, Jeremy told Gertie why he had returned to her without Miss Marney. They had quarrelled, he said, and the fault was his. *That*, Gertie did not doubt, though Jeremy spoke more with a sense of injury received than of injury done. With reasonable honesty, her nephew went on to say that they had not gone to the water garden but had followed the broad grass walk to the woodlands and then turned off on to a smaller path. It was there he had abandoned Elaine because she had threatened to scream if he did not leave her and had convinced him that she meant it.

Before Gertie could probe the reason Elaine had been driven to such an extreme, Miss Pilford parted from the friends to whom she had been talking and came back to them. There was nothing Gertie could do but show the girl an untroubled countenance and save her questions and her strictures for another time.

Guiltily aware of what he deserved, Jeremy turned all the power of his charm on Miss Pilford and offered to show her the water garden he had failed to show Elaine.

Miss Pilford had already visited this remarkable feature, but the handsome young guardsman had caught her interest, so she smiled up at him and declared it to be what of all things she would most like to see next. With a look towards Gertie that combined guilt, relief and triumph, Jeremy led Miss Pilford away.

Gertie watched them go with mixed feelings. Though not exactly a desirable event, a quarrel between Jeremy and Elaine need not be deplored if it finally detached her nephew from the girl. He had disappointed her by showing less sense than she had expected from him; certainly less than Elaine had shown in that particular case. But the possibility of Elaine being lost and unattended in these large, unfamiliar grounds was troubling. She must be found. And now where was Cato? How like a man not to be at hand when wanted!

'My dear Gertie, you look as though the world is treating you ill.'

Braxted's voice broke in on her thoughts and Gertie hastily summoned up a smile. 'Oh, it is a mere nothing.' But then as hastily corrected herself. 'No, there is something. Miss Marney became separated from Jeremy in the woodlands and is lost.'

While still at a little distance, Braxted had seen Jeremy walk away with Miss Pilford on his arm. Tactfully, he withheld the obvious questions of how Jeremy could, first, mislay a young lady and second, leave the woodland while she remained unfound. Obligingly, he offered to go in search of Miss Marney.

'It would be a kindness,' Gertie accepted. 'She is not familiar with these grounds and I should not like her to be distressed.'

Armed with the meagre directions Gertie was able to give him, Braxted walked off on his mission, amusing himself as he went with speculating on how Miss Marney came to be 'lost'. What appeared most likely was a quarrel between two young people and the probability was that it was Lazelle who had featured in Miss Marney's first, prohibited romance. A golden young man, of good family, not over-endowed with the world's goods, but who was in no way accustomed to being denied what he wanted. It would be interesting to know just how the quarrel had arisen and who felt the more aggrieved by it.

118

As he entered the woodlands it occurred to him that with such sketchy directions as he had, he could wander as long and as pointlessly as Miss Marney might be doing. Well, playing knight-errant to a schoolmaster's daughter was a novelty, at least. But the girl interested him, not only for her resemblance to her mother who still held a sad sweet place in his memory, but on her own account.

When the path was crossed by another, narrower and less well trodden, which was as far as Gertie's guidance extended, he assumed quarrelling lovers would seek privacy, decided between left and right, and turned left. . . .

Even when she had tidied her hair and replaced her bonnet Elaine had found she was still in need of time in which to cool both herself and her temper. For that reason she wandered slowly on along the winding, shaded path she and Jeremy had entered. She frowned over the recollection that twice now she had been kissed by a man without her consent. Given no time for thought in either case, her reactions had been curiously different. Her annoyance with Jeremy had been instant and unequivocal; her response to Cato Raffen had been less positive. It had begun with surprise, flowed into something close to pleasure before indignation had woken into life. But she surely owed Jeremy more tolerance than she owed Cato Raffen? It was a puzzling inconsistency.

A change in the light made her aware that the trees ahead were thinning and a moment or two later she walked into a wide grassy dingle. To her right, set on a slight mound backed by a high stone boundary wall, stood an ancient lattice arbour more than half-hidden under a creamy weight of roses. Sheltered by the wall and surrounding trees, stillness and warmth held the place as in a spell. The scent of the roses filled the hollow, hung heavily on the air, thick enough to daze the mind. As though drawn by an elfin lure of which the faint far off murmur of music was part, she walked towards the blossom-hung arbour.

Sitting deep in thought in the green, swimming light under the lattice and the roses, Cato did not see her strolling approach.

He had allowed Miss Marney's dislike of him to nettle him more than it usually did. Having left Gertie with her talkative cronies, he had walked away from the guests crowding the lawns and taken a roundabout path that had led him into the woods and his present solitude. His more usual response to Miss Marney's provocation was amused retaliation, but today he had failed to find amusement in it. And that was cause for further annoyance because it gave her too much importance. He admitted that, physically, she was more than a little attractive to him, but that was no good reason to allow her to make such wincing impact on his feelings. To shut her out of his mind now, he turned his thoughts to the Regent's affairs and to the Marquis of Braxted who made the link between himself and the prince.

He recalled with quizzical admiration the unshaken calm with which Braxted had listened to his tale of the dead seaman, at that time reposing in Ringlestones' tack-room. He had asked if Cato could name him and been told that he was almost certainly the smuggling brother of the groom who had sounded the alarm and the original source of information. It was likely that learning that information had been passed on had prompted the smuggler's extreme reaction. That in itself was a pointer to a path to be explored, but no more than that.

Braxted had accepted responsibility for disposal of the body with the same coolness as he had learned of its existence and followed acceptance with prompt action. The very next day, two neat and sober men had driven into Ringlestones' stable-yard in a covered wagonette. Asking no questions, quietly and efficiently, they had done what they came to do and driven away.

As imperturbable as the marquis, it seemed to Cato, Adam Kerby had watched the proceedings until the wagonette had driven out of the yard and then, without looking at his employer, said, 'Resurrection men. They'll have the clothes off him before they're out of the lane. Just in case.'

'Yes.' As Cato knew, unorthodox possession of a naked corpse as against a clothed one, made the difference in the eyes of the law between a misdemeanour and a felony, and so between imprisonment and hanging. But Cato had no expectation of the men facing either: Braxted, he felt certain, could be depended on for that. A man of parts. . . .

Elaine trod up the four steps of the arbour and was standing at the threshold before she became aware the place was occupied. When she did, in the elf-green gloaming, it took a moment more before she realized who was there.

Engrossed, Cato was as late to realize her presence. As he rose to his feet she began to speak and so did he. Both stopped and waited for the other.

'I did not know anyone was here,' she said lamely at last.

'And would have avoided the place like the plague if you had thought you would find *me*,' he said, his tone wry and sharp.

'With reason, I think.'

'And without it, too.'

There was no rancour in his voice this time; he was simply stating a fact. Elaine did not need better light to be sure his face wore its familiar wry smile. Turning away, she spoke across her shoulder, 'You have right of possession. I shall not stay to disturb you.'

'You disturb me whether you will or no, Miss Marney.'

That was true, he realized, and wished it unsaid. He never saw her without wanting to strike a response from her – and rarely achieved one that pleased him. It should not matter to him, as he had already informed himself. The trouble was that it did. The words seeming to speak themselves, he said, 'Don't go.'

Something in his voice made her hesitate, turn back.

He sensed she was still poised for flight, while he, having brought them to this point, had no idea how to take them on. The moment hung in delicate balance, long as eternity, heavy and sweet with promise.

Breaking the silence, a voice from somewhere behind Elaine said, 'Miss Marney, bowered in roses. A charming picture.'

With a short, jarring laugh, Cato stepped back into deeper shadow. 'I yield to rank,' he said. Then swiftly, differently, added, 'He cannot have seen me. Go out to him.'

Turning outward again, Elaine saw the Marquis of Braxted smiling up at her from a little distance. Slowly, reality began to come back to her. It was too unlikely a coincidence that the marquis was also here by chance and, because it would not do for her to appear to be keeping tryst with a man in a remote spot, for Gertie's sake as much as for her own, she walked down the steps towards him.

Confirming her thought that he had not come by chance, he said smilingly, 'The countess feared you lost and sent me to recover you from unnamed dangers. I was given directions but I confess I found you chiefly by good luck.'

Elaine smiled back at him, murmuring a vague acknowledgement as she laid a hand on the arm he offered. Unable to shake off the feeling that by his coming she had lost something of value – a discovery that might not offer itself again – she was blind to the anomaly of the Marquis of Braxted being despatched to look for her.

Braxted regarded her with interest. When she had first turned to him, he had taken the impression that for a moment or two she had not recognized him. She had looked like a dreamer

122

waking reluctantly. Certainly there had been nothing in her look
that hinted at a young woman sorrowing over a quarrel with her
lover. So, he thought, if she and Lazelle had fallen out, it was
Lazelle who had been the loser by it. More interesting to him was
the nature of the dream that had put that visionary look on the
girl's face. . . .

Through the lattice, Cato watched the two walk away, his gaze
chiefly on the slender figure in the amber-coloured gown. What
had he been trying to say to her when Braxted had made his
untimely appearance? A plea for friendship? He had made one
before – to no good end. Yet, for a few moments after he had
said 'don't go', he had sensed a difference in her; had thought he
had seen again something of the sweetness and vulnerability he
had once seen in her unconscious face. In those moments time
and intention had seemed to hang suspended . . . be mutable.

What beyond her desirability was her attraction for him? The
fact that he lusted after her was not enough to explain why she
came so often into his thoughts. But since he had no thought of
marriage and no intention of seducing Gertie's protégée, what
point was there to it?

The truth was she bedevilled him and that bedevilment was
complicated by the odd sense of responsibility he felt for her.
Conferred, it appeared, by the simple act of picking her up from
the floor of The Griffin. In return, too often, her green eyes
looked at him as though she saw him through a window made of
ancient glass that dimmed and distorted what she saw. *Why* it
seemed he was never to know.

His mood slipped towards the jaundiced. It was much ado
about nothing. He was not the only man to be attracted to her.
And if, as rumour had it, the Marquis of Braxted – long thought
to be immune to the charms of younger women – was looking
towards her—'

But *would* a Valdoe stoop to such a marriage? He paused on

the thought, then shrugged it aside. His responsibility to Miss Marney had no reality. Whatever the nature of Braxted's plans for Miss Marney's future, their fulfilment must surely depend on Miss Marney. . . .

CHAPTER ELEVEN

a day or two later, emerging from Hookham's Library in Bond Street with Polly Cutts, Elaine found their way blocked by a small crowd clustered round an elderly gentleman who had collapsed on to the flags. It was pointless to add to the number already attending him and Elaine began to edge a way around the group, only to be impeded by a man attempting the same manoeuvre in the opposite direction.

Recognition was instant – *Cousin Oliver!* Oliver looking prosperous in a dark, plum-coloured coat and an embroidered waistcoat in bright colours, much the same as he had worn at their first – and last – meeting. With a more knowledgeable eye than she had then possessed, she could see that the cut of the coat was a touch exaggerated, the buttons a shade too large and shiny, the waistcoat too gaudy.

Her instinct was to sweep past him, but a hackney carriage arriving to carry away the unfortunate gentleman and the movement of the surrounding crowd made it impossible.

Oliver's recognition of Elaine had been less immediate, but he was very quickly aware that the elegant young woman with whom he was face to face appeared to know *him*. His gaze swept down over her fashionable outfit and flowed up again to take in the face under the fetching bonnet of beige straw with gauzy white butterfly bows. It was the unfriendly gaze of her green eyes that gave him the clue to her identity.

Alley-cat eyes! he thought as he had thought at their first meeting. No longer a starving alley cat, though, but a cat that had landed on its feet and found the cream. What a transformation six or seven months had made. Not quite a beauty, yet little short of being one.

'Miss Marney. Cousin.' He swept off his hat and bowed. Excitement was already exploding in his mind as he realized that until this moment he had overlooked a sure and certain way of acquiring the wealth that was his constant goal. Hag-like as she had appeared that evening at The Griffin it was small wonder that it had not occurred to him that, by marrying her, Sarah's fortune would become his. At that time he had been too preoccupied with making sure he did not end up with a needy, unmarriageable female clutching at him for support. He had let her see his contempt, taken care to head off any demand the damned patronizing lawyer might make on her behalf. And then, when Woolford had made clear what the hoaxing words framing the will actually meant, it was too late. The miserable £500 for which at first he had been grateful but which had long since melted away, was nothing to what the lucky scarecrow was to have.

He had business here in London today, but he had come in the hope of finding luck, too. The sudden arrival of peace had upset his calculations, had suddenly closed off the most lucrative part of his carrier business; the very part that had contributed so handsomely to a standard of living he had come to regard as permanently established, the base from which further improvements were to be made.

For today's business he could thank his smuggling friends. It promised to be unusually rewarding, but it was not a kind likely to be repeated. That, he thought cheerfully, would matter nothing if he gained Sarah's fortune through marriage to his cousin.

Luck had indeed smiled on him. The leisured future he coveted suddenly appeared to be in reach and, as Cousin Elaine now looked, marriage to her would be no hardship.

Putting forward all the charm of manner he could command, he said, 'What a very pleasant surprise this is, Cousin. How much we must have to say to each other. Allow me to escort you to wherever it is you are going.'

'Thank you, sir, but I am not alone.' Elaine regarded him with distaste, her tone unencouraging.

Oliver took in the plainly dressed young woman standing in the background holding a parcel of what appeared to be books. A servant, of course. Another pointer to how far his prickly, green-eyed cousin had progressed – on money he could put to his own good use once it was in his grasp.

'But you will not deny me the pleasure of walking with you for a while?' he persevered.

'I would not think of taking you out of your way. We have not far to go.'

'So you are living in London now?'

'For the present.'

'And you are living where?'

Perhaps, Elaine thought a little desperately, Gertie's title would be enough to daunt his persistence. 'I am staying with the Countess of Sheffney!'

For a moment Oliver thought that could only be an invention to annoy or impress. But looking at her he saw he was wrong and at once was both impressed and annoyed. Starting from the condition in which he had first seen her, how the devil had she had risen so high?

'I am waited for, so I must ask you to excuse me, Mr Marney.' Elaine made another move to pass him.

Remaining solidly in her way, Oliver manufactured a smile. 'My name is Oliver, Cousin. For kinship's sake will you not use it? I have often regretted our having lost contact. We must not do so again. Allow me to know your address.'

With a hauteur she borrowed from one of Gertie's acquaintance, Elaine told him, 'Sheffney House, Berkeley Square, will find me,' and prayed that he found it impressive enough to daunt any intention he might have of calling on her. Adding a firm 'Good day, Mr Marney,' she made a more determined movement to pass him and this time Oliver thought it wise to stand aside.

Gazing after her with a simmering mixture of dislike, resentment and envy, Oliver promised himself future pleasure in curing her of her fine airs.

This second meeting with Oliver brought the first occasion storming back into Elaine's mind with all its attendant shocks and emotional turmoil. It was seven months since her great-aunt Sarah Marney's death had released her from a life of desperate penury and opened the way that had led her first into Fanny Woolford's warm and kindly sphere and then to Gertie's opulent, hedonistic world. Meeting Oliver again made her feel threatened, had left her with a sense of his having cast a shadow from the unhappy past on her.

The unsettled state of her mind was added to on her return to Sheffney House when she found Cato Raffen had called in her absence to tell Gertie that John Woolford, tracking through ancient archives, had found a document he was certain provided sufficient evidence to persuade his troublesome neighbour to withdraw his claim to any part of Ringlestones land. He had added power to the persuasion with the threat of a counter-suit for trespass.

'Clever John!' said Gertie. 'I knew if anyone could do it, he would. But Cato says now, that he has a buyer for the place who waits only for clearance of this matter to close the deal. I am sorry he cannot be turned from selling, but I must allow him to know his own business best. He will, of course, need money to restore Eldenshaw when it comes to him, but Ringlestones is both ancient and interesting. Not large but worth seeing. Cato invites us both to take a nuncheon with him there and look over the house before it changes hands. We are to go the day after tomorrow.'

Elaine was immediately torn between wanting to go and not wanting to go. The feeling that the interlude in the Relfords' arbour had left unfinished business between herself and Cato Raffen had not gone from her. The ambivalence of her response to the imminence of their next meeting came from not wanting to discover that Cato Raffen did not share that feeling. Why it was important to her she could not have said.

The visit was not to be avoided. She and Gertie set out for Richmond on the appointed day in warm sunshine, travelling in an open barouche, their complexions protected by parasols.

Gertie had visited the house before but not for some years and she remarked on the growth of the trees bordering the lane that led to Ringlestones' gates. The drive beyond these showed evidence of having been recently cleared of grass and weeds and the house at its end – a small timber-framed manor with mellow brick in-filling – sat snugly backed by its own woods, its heavy oak door hospitably open.

Cato came out to welcome them and the housekeeper, Mrs Stretton, a neat, competent-looking woman, was at hand in the panelled hall to show the ladies where they might leave their hats and scarves and freshen themselves after the journey.

Returning to where Cato waited for them, Gertie could not keep from making one last protest against the sale of the house. 'Seeing the place again, Cato, makes me wonder even more that you can bear to part with it. One cannot compare it with Eldenshaw, of course, but the staircase is very fine and the screen at the end of the hall . . . how many can there be half as pleasing?

'I have no use for the place, Gertie. And from what Landon, the doctor who attends Julian, last wrote me, it will not be long before I shall have Eldenshaw on my hands.'

'Oh!' Gertie regarded him gravely. 'Is the end so near? I will not tease you more, for I know you will then have enough and beyond to cope with. I'm glad to learn there is someone who troubles to keep you informed.'

Cato nodded agreement before changing the subject. 'I'm sure you must both be ready for some refreshment. Come this way to the dining-room and we'll see what Mrs Stretton has provided for us.'

The dining-room was another panelled room, long and low-ceilinged, made cheerful by the glow of a large crimson carpet that though a little worn in places showed the happy result of recent thorough cleaning.

Elaine found it hard to say anything. There had been no hint in Mr Raffen's look or manner that there had ever been a moment when it had seemed they had stood on the edge of a significant discovery. The illusion had been hers alone. As she took her seat at the table she took the resolve to keep a rein on her imagination and to concentrate on being a good guest. With that end in view, she made an effort and offered politely, 'The name Ringlestones has a pretty sound. Do you know how the house came by it?'

She looked up to see her host's eyes narrowed in unholy glee and knew her resolve was to meet its first test of the day.

'Yes, I do know – though I fear you will think less well of it when I tell you. It is named for the stones on which unfortunate pigs were used to have rings set in their noses. There are three such, supposedly of ancient use, let into the terrace on the south side of the house.'

Determinedly, she kept her face free of expression and said in the flattest of voices, 'Indeed. How interesting.'

His gaze sharpened wickedly. 'Yes, I thought you would find it sole

'Cato,' Gertie put in swiftly, 'your Mrs Stretton has provided a veritable feast. Surely she cannot have done so much without help?'

'I believe there are two, or even three, young handmaidens who scuttle around under her imperious rule.' He swept an arm towards the bountiful array of dishes. 'Now, what do you choose to begin with? The asparagus tart is a favourite of mine.'

The array before them was too tempting for the guests to be self-denying and justice was done to the recommended tart, the purée of mushrooms, cold fillets of salmon, almond creams and other dishes. Nor did the iced fruit punch and champagne they were offered go unregarded.

The meal was followed by tour of the house which, in addition to the handsome screen in the hall, had several other pleasing features, including a delightful fresco in the drawing-room and a very fine plastered ceiling in the principal bedroom.

Offered a tour of the grounds, Gertie declined, saying, 'Cato, I have eaten too much and at the wrong hour of the day. My feet will carry me no further than that very comfortable looking *chaise-longue* on which I mean to dispose myself to sleep for a while. If you and Miss Marney have energy to spare, then by all means expend it in walking round the grounds.'

Though feeling Gertie had betrayed her into an awkward situation, Elaine agreed to a walk. Making conversation with this most troublesome of men must surely be made easier with a varying scene to discuss than sitting in an enforced tête-à-tête with him.

The tilt of her parasol kept a small distance between them as they walked across the courtyard and took a path branching from the main drive towards the nearest of the encircling trees. Once in the shade however, her role as faultless guest required her to furl it.

131

Cato was determined not to tease Miss Marney further but had no great confidence that he would not. Breaking the silence that had fallen on them, he said formally, 'The grounds do not offer many visual delights, I fear, Miss Marney. It will take years to bring them to any sort of beauty. My cousin and his ancestors were mostly practically minded men, less concerned with beauty than with having good coverts for game, ponds for fish, orchards and kitchen gardens. Even those will take time to be restored to full usefulness. Long ago, there was a hermit's cell but a few stones buried under turf are all that remains of that. An ancient ice-house lurks somewhere beyond the kitchen gardens and not far from it, an antique dovecot housing a flight of baseborn pigeons. However, one thing of beauty I *can* show you and if we turn aside here, we'll find it just beyond those trees.'

Leaving the path where the trampled right-hand verge showed evidence of recent work, they walked between trees to arrive at a cleared space that once must have been a grassy circle. Scarred earth and trodden weed showed where saplings and brushwood had been removed. Central and solitary, in full magnificent flowering beauty, stood a tree of a kind that Elaine had never seen before. Sunlight set ablaze the flaunting orange at the base of each eight-inch, greenish-white pendant bell-like flower with which it was hung.

For several moments she did not speak. When she did it was to say softly, with warmth, 'It is beautiful beyond words!'

'I'm told it is a tulip tree from North America but who planted it and how they came by it, I don't know. Nor do I know why it should flourish so splendidly where it is.'

Impulsively, she swung round to him, her face alight with pleasure. 'Thank you for showing it to me.'

With rueful humour he said, 'Having won such success with the best I have, I am at a loss to know how to follow it.'

'You cannot. One perfect piece is enough. I am content.'

'Then so must I be.' He offered his arm and they began to retrace their footsteps in a serenely comfortable silence.

Reaching the path, they stopped as though undecided which way to go. The sun poured down its heat, the stillness was absolute, not a bird sang. As once before, it was as though the world waited on a particular and magical moment.

Lifting her gaze to his, Elaine found it held by the intensity with which Mr Raffen was looking at her. Her heart lurched queerly, began a faster rhythm, every nerve thrumming with a mysterious, expectant excitement.

His voice rough-edged, Cato said, 'Miss Marney?'

It was both a question and a statement, but her mind was not functioning and she understood neither. She simply stood gazing back at him, unable to help either him or herself.

Torn between exasperation and amusement, Cato wondered if she had the least idea of the turbulence she sent surging through him while she stood there apparently untroubled and unwrung. His gaze slid down to the tempting curve of her softly parted lips and succumbing to temptation, he gathered her into his arms and did what he had been wanting to do ever since the first half-dreaming kiss he had given her in Gertie's parlour.

Even so, he laid restraint on himself, began gently, his mouth tenderly persuasive – a lover's kiss. Only when her lips and body lost their rigidity, became pliant, yielding and finally responsive, with a soft grunt of triumph, he kissed her as the depth of his need demanded. Very soon, he was made aware that it was not enough . . . that it was necessary to set her attractions at a greater and less embarrassing distance. Hurriedly, he did so. Miss Marney, he saw, looked a little dazed.

Common sense returned with a chilling rush. Having done what he had so wanted to do, he could expect a reckoning. Society required men to keep a proper distance from its young unmarried women: such physical contact as he had just enjoyed

133

with Miss Marney called for the amend of a proposal of marriage – unless he was a rake, which he did not think he was. But he valued his freedom as much as any man and perhaps more because of the strong tug towards adventure now rooted in him. Marriage seemed to him a high price to pay for a kiss, or even two kisses, and he was already demurring at a cost that put his liberty at risk.

He had been a fool to indulge himself! Why couldn't he keep his hands off the girl! Self-preservation now demanded he find a way out of the hobble into which he had tied himself. Refusing to examine other thoughts and feelings astir at a deeper level, he spoke from those that lay on the surface, saying in amused tones, 'Propriety suggests I should make you a proposal of marriage following that delightful interlude, Miss Marney. I am aware, though, how little appeal such an offer – coming from *me* – would have for you, so I shall simply offer you my sincere thanks for what was a most pleasurable experience and hope you found equal pleasure in it.'

Elaine's shock at this cavalier pronouncement was all the greater for coming at a moment of joyous discovery, of wonder at her former blindness to her own feelings. Troublesome, perplexing as Cato Raffen was, he was the root cause of all her uncertainties. All along, she had fought against recognizing the strength of her attraction to him. But under that, and more to be reckoned with, there had grown a passion of feeling for him never suspected.

His words brought her to earth with a jolt, scorched everything from her mind but the one thought: he believed her response to his kisses had been an attempt to trap him into marriage. . . . She was riven by self-disgust. How could she think of love in connection with this most arrogant of men! But she hadn't *thought*, she raged at herself. She had allowed her surprised senses to take control and in doing so made herself, once again, a target for his mockery.

It did not occur to her that, less quick to give recognition to deeper emotions, he had floundered into crass gracelessness. The wound to her feelings was deep. Drawing on every reserve she possessed to hide it from him, she said with a lightness more brittle than his had been, 'You are right, of course, in thinking I should find the idea of a marriage between us too ill-judged to contemplate. Though I admit a momentary lapse into folly, I am not entirely without sense.' She gave him a glittering smile and turned back on the path. 'I think we should return to the house.'

He had been put in his place, dismissed. He began to wonder how his self-protecting words had sounded to her; to wonder if they had done damage. He caught up with her, laid his hand on her arm. 'I beg you will allow me to say—'

Her glance scornful, she cut across his words. 'No, Mr Raffen. No further words are needed. We have arrived at a fair understanding. I have been aware for some time of your contempt for me, but spare me further expression of it.'

Astonished into silence – where had she got that idea? – Cato allowed her to go ahead. When at last he began to follow, it was in a simmer of guilt and vexation.

More disturbing and deeper than either, was a sense of loss.

CHAPTER TWELVE

Elaine fought the pain she would not accept she felt with angry bitterness following her return from Ringlestones. The kisses she had exchanged with Cato Raffen lived in her memory with deep shame for having allowed herself to be beguiled into thinking even for a moment that his could have had any sincerity of feeling behind them. In forgetting the lessons of the past, she had laid out her pride for him to savage, had led him to think she was hoping to trip him into marrying her.

The thought of her stupidity was unbearable. Above all, she hated herself for having thought she loved him. At twenty years of age she was old enough to recognize that the romance that had attended Gertie's meeting with her husband was rare: Gertie had simply been fortunate beyond reasonable everyday expectation.

The arrival of a charming bouquet from Oliver and a letter that proclaimed his delight in having renewed acquaintance with her and his hope of calling upon her before too long were both forgotten within minutes of their reaching her.

She was unpleasantly reminded within a week. It was late one afternoon when the last of the more usual callers had gone that Oliver was shown into the drawing-room where she and Gertie were still sitting. His name and his claim to cousinship had gained him entry.

Elaine regarded him with unfriendly eyes and met him with chilly courtesy, introducing him of necessity to Gertie. It had been a mistake, she realized, not to have taken more notice of his overtures and to think he would not pursue beyond the doors of Sheffney House whatever purpose he had in mind. She saw he had done his sartorial best for the visit and had come as near to a gentlemanly appearance as he was likely to achieve. Though possessed of powerful shoulders, his figure had nothing clumsy about it and his dark blue coat was sober enough for church, though she doubted it would be seen there. His waistcoat was a not-too-gaudy silk tabard and his linen could not be faulted.

Oliver was not himself particularly pleased with the sobriety of his appearance, but he was satisfied that he presented the appearance of solid worth for which he had tried.

He was not in awe of Gertie's rank but the grandeur of Sheffney House was so far out of his previous experience as to impose a restraint on his manner that helped the impression he wanted to make. Aware of the coolness of his reception, he placed the blame where it belonged.

Even now, at this his third meeting with Elaine, he had difficulty connecting the vivid, elegant girl before him with the gaunt, half-witted creature he had encountered in The Griffin. That he had made a bad mistake at that time, he knew, but how could anyone have possibly guessed that the crack-brained old harridan, their great-aunt, could have prepared such a shock for them as she had in leaving a solid fortune behind her? Or that it would go in its entirety to the girl with his portion only the miserable sum which had provided the income on which the pair had subsisted until the time of Sarah's death? Who could be surprised he had thought the girl feeble-minded when she had received the news of her inheritance in a flood of tears before bolting out of the room like a wild woman?

Shrewdly, he made putting himself in Gertie's good graces his first object and was moderately successful. Under his careful politeness, however, he was afire with impatience for Her Ladyship to leave him alone with his cousin so that he might discover whether she had a bridegroom in prospect yet, or whether he could hasten things on by beginning an approach to her that would lead to matrimony and Sarah Marney's fortune.

Conversation meandered along for twenty minutes or so until Gertie, deciding that, though a rough diamond, Oliver was respectable enough to be trusted alone with his cousin for a short time, tactfully excused herself.

Relaxing, Oliver cast an admiring glance around the room and remarked, 'A very different habitation from Great-aunt Sarah's hovel, Cousin. You must find it a famous thing to be so finely established.' A famous thing, indeed! he thought enviously. How the devil had she managed it? The nobs didn't usually take the likes of himself and Elaine Marney into their homes.

Elaine inclined her head and said nothing.

Oliver edged his chair nearer to hers and smiled ingratiatingly at her. 'Well, as your only male relative – your only relative of any kind, in fact – it is natural I should feel some responsibility towards you. Believe me, Cousin, I shall always be ready to advise or assist you in any way I can.'

With a clear memory of how swift he had been to head off any possible claim for help Mr Woolford might make on her behalf on the night of Sarah's funeral, Elaine accepted his words for what they were worth, wondering only what had brought about this present appearance of concern for her.

She was soon enlightened.

'Great-aunt Sarah's mad-brained sort of will makes it devilish awkward for me to speak to you of marriage. But it's what all you young ladies look for, isn't it? Marriage, I mean. But Sarah put you in a real fix where that's concerned, didn't she? Not but what you're not pretty enough to draw a man to you. . . . Maybe you've already found a man rich enough not to trouble about a lack of dowry?' He gave her an arch look of enquiry.

How stupid of her not to have recollected how Oliver would benefit by her marriage! How could it be other than of first importance to him. The wonder was that he had not made earlier enquiry.

'No,' she said very coolly, 'I cannot claim so much.'

Oliver leaned across to capture one of her hands. 'Never you mind. Without a doubt, you'll find a sensible man yet to marry you, one day. Meanwhile, you and me can be friends. We're cousins, so it's quite proper for us to come to first names. We'll be Elaine and Oliver from now on.'

Looking away from the blaze of his blue eyes, she found herself gazing down at the hand which held hers. For the first time she noticed how large and powerful-looking it was with black hair sprouting on the first joints of the spatulate fingers and showing more beneath the cuff-frill of his shirt. For some reason she shivered.

'Oliver?' he insisted coaxingly.

'Yes, very well – Oliver,' she agreed pulling her hand from his, finding it an effort not to snatch, wishing he would go.

Satisfied he had made a fair beginning, Oliver obliged her as soon as the countess came back into the room. To Elaine, speaking with care again, he said, 'I don't stay long in London this visit but shall write to you in hope of being favoured with your news now and then, Cousin Elaine. To this address.' He handed her a card with a Tunbridge Wells address on it.

Taking it, Elaine allowed him to assume her willingness and drew a deep sigh of relief when the door closed on him.

Silence settled heavily on the room until Gertie asked, 'You were not expecting your cousin to call?'

'No.'

'And do not care for the acquaintance?'

'No. Before today I had met him only twice. The second occasion was recent and no more than a brief and accidental encounter in the street. The first occasion however, was sufficiently instructive to have a lasting effect.'

She saw Gertie's look sharpen at her tone and went on to give her a tersely worded outline of what had happened at that first meeting.

Gertie listened attentively, trying to build a clear picture of what had happened, trying to think of what would be most helpful to say. When Elaine came to the end, she offered, 'You were in a very low state of health at that time, I remember Fanny telling me. Had suffered shock on shock. Is it possible you did not see things quite as they were? Or felt too strongly about them? Mr Marney is your only remaining relative, you say. He seemed to show a proper regard for you today and I cannot help but feel that you should not reject his acquaintance out of hand. It must be so very sad to be entirely without family.' Knowing only the warmth of an affectionate family.' Gertie felt that even the least congenial relative must have value.

Elaine had no doubt that she had seen Oliver in his true light, but not wishing to appear to repudiate Gertie's advice, murmured what might be taken for agreement.

'Take time to consider the matter,' Gertie concluded. 'If, in the end, you don't wish to see him that is easily arranged. It shall be as you wish.'

An Alvanley ball was as little to be missed as any given by the Duchess of Richmond and very soon after Gertie and Elaine's arrival, Lieutenant Dacier presented himself to Miss Marney as a hopeful partner.

Since the Hyde Park adventure he had shown increasing attention to Elaine though it had not yet reached the point at which he might be looked on as a suitor, but Gertie had made a mental note that she would be wise to make discreet enquiries of the Stapfords regarding his circumstances. The Stapfords themselves were an old, wealthy and respected family, which was recommendation enough for the time being.

Elaine found the lieutenant both charming and amusing. Far from attempting to turn to account his rescue of her, he continued to insist that he saw it only as a matter of good fortune that he had been in the right place at the right time. She enjoyed his company and welcomed him with pleasure whenever he approached her.

Because an Alvanley ball was so well regarded, guests tended to arrive earlier than was generally usual and it was still early evening when the the Marquis of Braxted joined Gertie and Elaine. At that time the ballroom was comfortably full; additions to the number would threaten comfort.

It had not taken Gertie's anxiety to make Braxted aware of society's interest in the attentions he showed Elaine and he was careful to limit their public showing. But she was a magnet to his interest. In the beginning the reason for his notice had lain in the past, but very soon he had been surprised to find he was drawn to her for reasons that were all her own. She was a pleasure to be with, a pleasure to look at. He approved her self-possession and the absence of calculation in her attitude towards himself, his rank and his wealth. It was some time since he had danced with her but tonight he was allowing himself the indulgence: 'If', as he said smiling down at her, 'you will allow me the pleasure?'

Elaine was never short of partners and he had to wait for two dances to be completed before he could lead her out. Before long, he sensed a change in her. Nothing great, but the sparkle was a little dimmed, her smiles came less easily.

'Do I detect a certain gentle melancholy in you tonight, Miss

Marney?' he asked presently. 'Are you suffering the common malaise of young people of being crossed in love?'

The question had not been serious, but her too-quick denial suggested he had come close to truth.

Her 'Oh, no!' had been too immediate, too fierce, Elaine realized at once. Colour rose in her cheeks and trying for a recover, she said as airily as she could, 'I'm not as young as *that*!'

'Are you so long out of the schoolroom then?'

'Longer than you think, I suspect, sir.'

That had come out very drily and had not invited further questions. They danced in silence for a while and when they spoke again it was mere chat and Braxted saw she was making an effort to shake off her low spirits. He wondered who the man was. *Not*, he thought, young Lazelle who was seen everywhere these days with Miss Pilford. He had taken particular note of the way she had looked at the pair on one occasion and there had been something almost teasing in her gaze when it met Lazelle's. As though, he had thought then, she had at some time foretold a change of heart on his part.

The dance ended and they began to walk slowly towards where they had left Gertie but turned aside to examine a side-table with a top of exquisitely inlaid marble.

'It's beautiful,' Elaine said.

'And new to this house,' Braxted said, running his fingers lightly over the surface. 'Or newly placed here. Florentine for a guess, and an object to covet.'

They were turning from the table when a boisterous young couple collided with Elaine, apologized hastily and rushed on. The knuckles of the hand that held Elaine's fan and handkerchief had struck hard against the edge of the marble top and her fingers made nerveless, she dropped both.

Braxted bent to retrieve them, but when about to hand them to her, paused to look closer at the flowered-wreathed embroi-

143

dered initials in one corner of the lace-edged scrap of lawn.

Idly curious, he said, 'E.L.M. The L stands for what?'

'Luce.' She spelt it, adding, 'Pronounced *loose*, not Lucy as people generally expect.'

Her answer had an odd effect on Braxted. He stood motionless, staring at her for several long moments. When at last he returned his gaze to the handkerchief stretched between his fingers almost to the point of tearing, he said in a harsh voice, 'You are nineteen, are you not?'

'I am twenty, sir.'

'Gertie told me— I am certain Gertie told me you were nineteen.'

'My twentieth birthday was a week or two after I joined her. She could not have known that.'

'So you were born in 1794?' he said in the same trenchant tone.

'Yes. On the 4th of May.'

His head lifted and he gazed unsmiling at her puzzled face. 'There is something I should have told you before, perhaps. I knew your father. He was my tutor. He—'

But while they were absorbed in what was passing between them, someone had been pushing through the crowd to find Braxted. A change had come over the guests, too. A strange excitement had compacted them into whispering groups; an excitement that did not breed laughter, but rather seemed to have slain it. The man who came to Braxted's side had the look of a confidential secretary and appeared to be known to the marquis who, with a hasty apology to Elaine, stepped aside to receive whatever message the man was so plainly anxious to convey.

In a short while, Braxted nodded assent to whatever was proposed and the man turned and left as purposefully as he had come. To Elaine, Braxted said, 'We must find Gertie and then, I'm sorry, but I must leave you.'

Gertie had been in close conversation with Princess Lieven but the two women parted before Braxted and Elaine reached her.

'You've heard?' Braxted asked Gertie without preamble.

'Yes. The princess told me. If true, it is a serious matter isn't it?'

'If true, it is a threat to the stability of the throne.' His gaze picked out the princess on her way out of the room among a group of men and a few other women who were also leaving. 'Dorothea will be on her way to Carlton House, which is where I must now go. If and when there is news, I will send word either here or to Sheffney House, depending on the hour. I imagine you will remain a while yet?'

Gertie nodded and Braxted said his goodbyes and left.

Elaine could hardly wait to ask Gertie what had happened. 'Obviously it concerns the Regent,' she said. 'But surely all who have left cannot be going to Carlton House?'

'No. Some will, of course, because those leaving are mainly the politicos and the political hostesses. But some will gather where they are accustomed to meet those who share their political persuasion. A great many will go to Connaught House.'

'Where the Regent's wife lives. . . . But what has *happened*?'

'Let us go to the supper-room and sit down where we can talk in peace and I will tell you. I imagine there will be little dancing for a while.'

When they were settled, Gertie said, 'What has happened follows on from the rumpus of two days ago when Princess Charlotte summoned the Prince of Orange to Warwick House and told him their betrothal was at an end. The Regent is not one to stomach such defiance and while the Princess was away from her home today, he went there and made a clean sweep of all her ladies-in-waiting, including her close friend Miss Margaret Mercer and her lady companion, Miss Cornelia Knight. Charlotte returned to find ladies of her father's choice installed in their place.'

145

'Oh dear! And they say she is as impatient of opposition as is the Regent. What did she do?'

'She rushed into the street, hailed a common hackney cab and was driven to her mother at Connaught House. As sovereign prince, His Highness would not – could not – follow her there. And Charlotte is eighteen now and so, as a *royal*, is of age. What will come of the breach hardly bears thinking of, because Dorothea Lieven says Charlotte is determined to rid herself of the Prince of Orange at all costs.

'What will the Regent do? What *can* he do in such a situation?'

'He will see that every possible pressure is put on the Princess to persuade her to return to her own home. But she is young and has never been easily ruled. By now, too, she must be feeling the power of her position and has not yet learned the restraints of responsibility. It is a dangerous situation. The Princess is popular and the Regent is not. You have experienced at first hand the power of the mob. If this leaks out to the common people and they see Charlotte as a victim of her father's bullying, there will be terrible riots and heaven knows what the end would be. There is discontent over many things in the country and this could be enough to set us on the same road as was taken by France in the days of the Terror.'

And that, Elaine knew, was a lingering and genuine fear in the minds of the aristocracy.

The ball went on with rumours from various sources filtering in to provide slightly hectic stimulation as they were interpreted and reinterpreted. What became clearer with each hour that passed was that the key to the deadlock was in Princess Charlotte's hands. At three in the morning Gertie and Elaine were driven back to Sheffney House.

Neither Gertie nor Elaine had long risen from their beds when Braxted presented himself.

146

The crisis was over, he told them, and for that both Prince and country might thank the least regarded among the procession of the great and the good who had had made their way to Connaught House in the hope of ending the Princess's determination to remain in her mother's house, something the Regent had long ago prohibited. Foremost in importance among those who had gathered at Connaught House was the Archbishop of Canterbury. After him came the Princess's favourite uncles, the Dukes of York and Sussex, the Lord Chancellor, several of her dismissed ladies. Low in the scale of importance, had come Mr Brougham. He was not a member of the Tory government, but a Whig, and at the time, could not even claim the distinction of a seat in Parliament. He was also a lawyer and so was despised by some as an upstart. A clever man, he was known to be sympathetic to Charlotte.

Through the long night the young Princess used her power with increasing confidence. She received only those whom she chose to see and remained unmoved by argument, exhortation or persuasion into any thought of returning to her own house and so, effectively, returning to her father's control.

Nearing five in the morning, Mr Brougham was admitted to her presence. In a little while he prevailed on her to go with him to the window and look out on the streets that dawn was beginning to lighten. Soon, he said, those streets would be filled by people. If he drew their attention to her standing there and told them her grievances Carlton House, her father's home, would be attacked, torn down even, the soldiers would be called out, blood spilled. And it would not be forgotten in a hundred years that her running away was the cause. . . .

Then, at last, the Princess agreed to return to Warwick House – but not before ensuring recognition of her utter refusal to marry the Prince of Orange.

Braxted lapsed into weary silence at the end of his story. He had not yet been to bed and Elaine thought that for the first time he looked his age.

Rousing himself, he finished, 'Poor Slender Billy will, no doubt, leave us as quietly as he came, having had shabby treatment all along the line. Charlotte may yet do worse for herself. There are not too many among the eligibles as pleasant and good-natured as he is.'

He stood up. 'I must leave you, or I shall fall asleep before your eyes.'

'How did His Highness take it all?' Gertie asked, rising, too.

'As you may imagine, not lightly. It might have been easier for him if he could have blamed Princess Caroline as the instigator of it all, but that wasn't possible.' He shook his head, adding with tired cynicism, 'He will, of course, be elected villain of the piece as usual. What can the man ever do that will be considered right?'

It was only after he had gone that Elaine remembered that, at the ball, the marquis had started to tell her about his connection with her father when he had been interrupted by news of the royal scandal.

CHAPTER THIRTEEN

A letter from the Earl of Sheffney to his wife informing her he now had hope of returning to England within a week or two, put Gertie in high good humour. Twenty years of marriage had not damped her enthusiasm for her husband's company and her caustic 'About time, too!' when she had read the letter did not deceive Elaine who saw the flare of pleasure Her Ladyship's eyes.

Elaine was reminded, however, that time was passing, that the purpose for which Gertie had invited her to London was to find a husband. Was this the spur all indigent young women felt towards the end of a hard-won season? The barb prodding them into accepting *any* man who made a belated offer? She could not see a likelihood of even that happening in her case and for that reason, she could be thankful that remaining unmarried did not mean inevitable penury. Coldly unattractive to her though spinsterhood was, it was preferable to feeling forced into marriage with a man simply because none other had offered it.

Gertie now began to talk of removing to Bredescourt, her home in Surrey and seat of the Earls of Sheffney for the better part of three centuries, and Elaine decided it was time to set a term to her stay at Sheffney House. Gertie swept the idea purposefully aside.

'Nonsense! Sheffney's return is no cause for you to fly from us.

Never mind that the right suitor has not yet put himself forward. It is not as if no man has been attracted to you. There have been several enquiries. All very discreet, of course, but with an obvious purpose. There is no escaping the fact, however, that a lack of dowry is a very considerable handicap. For all that, you need not despair. You must come with us to Bredescourt. Our neighbourhood is not without a bachelor or two and Dorking town is at no great distance.' She gave Elaine a quizzical look. 'I cannot let you go yet. Fanny would not let me hear the end of it if I fail to find you a husband. And one as satisfactory to her as to you.'

Conscious of how much she owed Gertie, Elaine found it difficult to stand out against her happy certainty of Elaine's compliance. She wanted to say that she had not thought deeply enough before embarking on a search for a husband; that doubts had crept in to alter her feelings; that she wanted—

There she ran aground. Less than ever did she know what she wanted. Or if she did, she dared not give it recognition. . . .

Gertie – planning ahead – was thinking that though it had been a great pity that Matthew Gifford's mother had so ill-timed her departure from life as to prevent her son coming to London this particular year, there was still hope of him. There could be nothing against his making a private visit. He had never been averse from visiting Bredescourt and living as he did in the same county, distance was no obstacle. Then, too, Lieutenant Dacier appeared in no great hurry to return to his own country and might be happy to spend a few weeks in Surrey. . . .

The furore over Princess Charlotte's rebellious stand on her grievances had died away and society was now amusing itself trying to predict who would fill the vacancy left by the Prince of Orange.

The Regent, mindful of the common people's right to share in the victory celebrations and make merry in their own way, had planned lavish entertainment for them in the public parks.

Some members of society who chose to view the extravaganzas reported them with a fashionable sneer, but with the ordinary citizenry they were a huge success with just enough going wrong to lend extra interest and heighten excitement. The widely advertised balloon ascent, after a patience-trying delay, was as impressive as intended, though the balloon came down far off course, sixteen miles below Gravesend in Mucking Marsh and only the cool-headedness of the balloonist having averted disaster. The model ships on the water in Hyde Park caught fire; in St James's Park the seven-storey pagoda built on the Chinese Bridge not only caught fire, but tilted and some of its fireworks went astray causing accidents. But in Green Park, the chief showpiece, the Citadel of Concord was a triumph, transforming magically from a fort to a temple of peace behind a veil of smoke. Around it all, the parks were fairylands of Chinese lanterns and variegated lights, while bands scattered throughout the acreage provided music for dancing.

Ignoring the successes, the mischances lent venom to the pen of that most malicious of satirical versifiers, Mr John Wolcot. A sometime doctor writing behind the name of Peter Pindar, he had made himself the scourge of the Regent who was the chief butt of his scurrilous wit.

When the shows in the parks were at an end, the citizenry proved reluctant to let the carnival go. In Hyde Park, drinking booths proliferated, an illicit fair was set up and rowdyism grew apace. The chancellor had ordered an immediate end but it was five days before the now grassless park could be cleared.

On 9th August, the Regent, unthanked for his efforts, was given relief from the chief of his many tribulations when his wife, Princess Caroline, quietly left the country to begin a less quiet tour of Europe which, whatever the truth of her behaviour, added no credit to her reputation.

Oliver had seen the sights, but his chief object in again being in London was to establish his courtship of Elaine. Progress, if any, was slow and was a strain on the impatience natural to him. Accustomed to success with women, however, he did not doubt his ultimate victory. It was the waste of his time that provoked him.

It was long since he had had to plod beside the wide iron-shod wheels of a carrier's wagon, though he had done his resentful share in his father's day. He had been sixteen when his father died of an apoplexy and the business had come under his command. No fool, but young enough to take risks, he had seen the strength and importance of the smuggling trade and established a dependable connection with it. His business had prospered and expanded. Now he only undertook such journeys as required speed, or had special importance, and these he made either on horseback or in a hired travelling chaise.

But he was hungry for greater success, for the certainty of a fortune behind him and a life of gentlemanly ease before him. So he walked softly around Elaine and the Countess of Sheffney and did his best to please. Underneath there was a growing resentment that it should be necessary to expend so much charm and restraint. Elaine was, after all, no more than a means to an end and once that end was achieved he would see she paid for the strain she put on his patience.

Frustration was leaching at Cato's patience, too – and from two directions.

It seemed to him that every meagre clue he uncovered took him very little further towards identifying the Regent's would-be assassin. That the vital piece of knowledge lay somewhere between Hampshire, London and the Kent coast gave him a wide area of search and already he had followed more tortuous and frustrating paths than could be easily tolerated. Though, as he had told Gertie, he had a direction in which to look, he was left with too many candidates and no key to the puzzle on which to fix.

He saw the passing of time as daily increasing the Regent's danger, but suspected that Braxted thought the crucial point had been passed when the Prince had been shot at in Hyde Park. Braxted appeared to have some other preoccupation. He had gone out of town and left no word as to when he might be expected to return. Cato, however, was as certain as ever that the man he sought still stalked the Regent with murderous intent.

Since the day before the Regent had been shot at, when a warning note had been pushed into his hand by a ragged urchin who had immediately scampered off, he had known that he himself was at risk. He believed it to be written in a genuinely illiterate hand, but he did not believe the warning to have originated from the writer. *That*, he was sure, came from the assassin himself – and for no quixotic reason.

To have the memory of what had happened between himself and Elaine Marney at Ringlestones thrusting across his concentration with distracting frequency was more than a vexation. He had done damage, he knew, and did not want to be reminded of it. Though there had come a point at which Miss Marney had accepted his kisses, had even begun to return them, her inexpertise remained with him as a reproach. And when, to save them both embarrassment, he had set her at a little distance, there had been something in her expression that had touched his heart. Then he, in defence of his prized liberty, with crass and perverse clumsiness, had shattered whatever dream had been waking in her mind.

From the time he had met her in Woolford's library at Bellehaugh, she had amused, provoked and interested him. To discover that beneath that pull, there was now a wellspring of tenderness for her, an aching desire to protect and cherish her, was a matter for dismay. Because if those were elements of love,

153

then he loved her. And what could be more foolish when it so little suited him to be trammelled? Loving limited one's freedoms, made demands.

Miss Marney for her part, had made it abundantly clear that any further attempt on his part to mend matters would only worsen them. Once free of his present commitment to the Regent's preservation, he would be wise to take himself off to Wiltshire, back to India, *anywhere* that put a forbidding number of miles between them.

Which conclusion hardly accorded with his setting out for Sheffney House some time later with a small packet in his pocket.

The stiff civilities exchanged between Elaine and Cato when goodbyes were said at Ringlestones, had alerted Her Ladyship to a further falling out between the two. Elaine had not confided in her and for that reason she had hesitated to quiz her about it. Where Cato was concerned, she felt she had a sisterly right to do so and Elaine being safely absent on a visit to Miss Pilford, she waited impatiently for opportunity, then demanded in a rallying way, 'Tell me, Cato, what *is* it that sets you and Elaine forever at odds with one another?'

Without thought, he snapped back, 'The fact that she has disliked me from the start.'

Gertie frowned. 'It is not like her to take someone in unreasonable aversion. Did you give her cause?'

He shrugged. 'I don't know. Not intentionally. I have sometimes teased her a little since, but her dislike came first.'

'I cannot believe her so unreasonable. And something happened between you at Ringlestones. Something beyond a little teasing, I think.'

He was silent so long she thought she had ventured too far and he did not mean to answer her. But then, explosively, he said, 'If you will have it, at Ringlestones I gave her good reason for dislike. Not intentionally: sheer clumsiness from being off balance.

'But how? Why?'

'Why? Because I'm a fool! How? Because having thoroughly kissed her, I said enough and in a manner to give any woman reason to take exception.'

'Oh, Cato! That is well beyond teasing. So wrong! So improper! What were you about?'

Cato sprang to his feet, strode away from where they sat, came back. 'Because I find it hard to keep my hands off her! Because I'm in love with the girl and I don't want to be. I've tried not to admit it to myself and would rather not have had to admit it to you. And there you have it!'

Gertie closed her eyes, shook her head. 'I have so hoped that would not happen. You know you cannot afford to marry her even if she were willing.'

He looked at her in surprise. 'Lack of fortune's no bar. Have I not told you? I'm not the indigent being I was when I left these shores ten years ago. I chanced to be in the position to save the life of an Indian prince on one eventful occasion. Such princes value themselves highly and show their appreciation of such a signal service in proportion – almost literally, by weight of gold and precious stones. To decline to be rewarded would be to offer unforgivable insult, belittling the value of the life saved. So, with other accretions, I am happy to say, my dear Gertie, that I am passing rich.'

'Well. . . .' Gertie gazed at him speechlessly while she adjusted her ideas to the difference this must make to him. When at last she spoke, it was with warmth and sincerity. 'I cannot tell you how glad I am to hear it, Cato. It changes everything for you. You will be able to restore Eldenshaw and with the rank you will one day have, you may look higher for a bride than once you could. That is something you should not overlook.'

He shrugged that aside impatiently. 'There is only one woman I would consider marrying and that is Elaine Marney and I have made sure I am the last man she would take as a husband.'

'Then you are in hopeless case, my friend, and would be wise to look elsewhere. I must warn you that Braxted is still showing interest in that direction. Unlikely as I have thought it, it *is* possible he has marriage in mind. Lieutenant Dacier, too, has been very attentive of late.'

It was not what he wanted to hear. With dry savagery, he said, 'No doubt either would make her a better husband than I should.' He put a hand in a pocket and drew out the small packet. 'May I leave this with you to deliver to Miss Marney? She shared a philippina with me when I dined at your sister's house and I had thought to redeem it with this trifle. She may do with it as she pleases.'

He stood for a moment as though at a loss, then said abruptly, 'I shall take myself off, being no fit company for you or anyone.'

CHAPTER FOURTEEN

*G*ertie was still thinking over what Cato had told her when Elaine looked into the room to show her return. Beckoning her in, she held out the packet that had been left with her.

'From Cato Raffen. He called while you were out.'

Elaine took the packet from her as though it might explode and stood looking down at it without making any attempt to remove its covering.

Unable to gauge the girl's reaction, Gertie said with smiling impatience, 'Oh, do open it! If you do not wish to see what it is, *I* do.'

Slowly, Elaine untied the tape and folded back the tissue to reveal a small round ivory box, about two inches in diameter and about the same in height. The lid was carved into a slightly flattened replica of a water-lily, perfect in every exquisite detail. This removed to show sitting on the bottom of the box and part of it, a hopeful-looking little frog, equally perfect and seeming only to wait to leap out.

'I don't understand,' Elaine said flatly. 'Why should Mr Raffen give me a present?'

'It seems you shared a philippina, a twin-kernelled nut, when you both dined with John and Fanny. There is a nonsensical little custom observed by those who know it, for a gentleman to make the lady who shares her nut with him a small gift.' She took the box from Elaine's hand to look at it, saying as she handed it back, 'It really is quite delightful.'

'Yes,' Elaine agreed stiffly. Delightful. And one more thing to set her teeth on edge where Cato Raffen was concerned. And perhaps meant to be so. Leaving Gertie to put what interpretation she chose on the philippina's reception, she carried the box away with her to her bedroom.

There, she set it down on the polished surface of the mahogany chest of drawers. She wasted another moment or two staring at it as though it might yield some clue to the mind of the giver, but nothing came to her. She did not understand him. Nor did she understand herself, or by what treacherous path she had come to think even for a moment that she loved him. It was a piece of folly for which she could not even have the satisfaction of blaming him, for what encouragement had he ever given her?

She could be thankful her foolishness had been so brief. It would not be repeated. But now she was left with the unwelcome task of writing to thank him. . . .

For two days the water-lily box swam above its own reflection in the shining wood of her chest. By the third day it had become so much a source of annoyance, she shut it away in a drawer.

The London season which normally ended early in July had already stretched into August in this exceptional year. Returning from a shopping trip to Burlington Arcade to purchase silk stockings and sundry other items for herself and Gertie, Elaine, with Polly in attendance, was nearing Berkeley Square when a curricle swept round a corner at great speed, swung wide and crashing against a bollard, overturned.

Though accidents were commonplace in the capital's crowded

streets, they were much less so in this quiet locality. The occupants, two young men and a bantam-weight groom were thrown from the vehicle as the wheel that had taken the brunt of the impact collapsed in ruin. The frightened horses careered on dragging the wreck halfway down Dover Street before coming to a trembling stand.

Calling to Polly to follow her, Elaine hurried across to the prostrate figures. Driver and passenger had been thrown on to the pavement and both were unconscious. The groom, who had been acting as tiger, was making feeble movements to sit up but looked white and dazed. An ominous amount of blood was spreading from beneath the head of the curricle's driver and Polly, coming up to Elaine, turned almost as white as the groom. Dropping the parcels she was carrying, she clapped a hand to her mouth and wailed, 'Oh, Miss!'

'Don't you dare fail me now!' Elaine told her brusquely. as she knelt down beside the driver. 'Find the package with the length of nightdress lawn I bought and tear off a strip.' Warily she lifted the young man's head to see the damage but his hair was thick and curly, making it difficult to tell how badly his skull was damaged. She wondered why no one from the nearest house had come to offer help when she saw the knocker was off the door and realized the family was absent.

As soon as Polly had handed her a strip of linen, she wadded it into a pad to put under the driver's head, saying worriedly, 'We need help. And an apothecary. Knock at one of the doors and ask someone to come.'

The second young man, though barely conscious, was beginning to moan now. Distractedly aware of her inability to attend to them all at once, or even to treat *one* of them with any real competence, she prayed for help. How could any street be so entirely empty so late in the morning? Then, with relief, she heard first the rattle of wheels abruptly halted and next the sound of hurrying footsteps. A moment later, a recognizable presence was both helping and giving knowledgeable advice. She was too occupied, too grateful for intelligent support, to react to who it was helping her before Polly at last brought other assistance, and the news that an apothecary had been sent for.

Relieved of responsibility, Elaine was helped to her feet by her timely Jack-at-a-pinch. She gazed at him in a dazed sort of way, feeling shaken and a little sick now that her part in the emergency was over.

Regarding her with smiling approval, Cato wondered how any young woman in a grimy, bloodstained dress, her bonnet hanging by its ribbons at her back and her hair in a tangle, could look so appealing. Impulsively and with a sincerity that could not be doubted. he said, 'You, Miss Marney, are a most remarkable young woman and I wish with all my heart you would forgive me my sins!'

The tribute passed her by, but the tone of his words somehow struck through all the knots and twists of past encounters and held her waiting, unreasonably ready to do as he asked.

Her look – thoughtful, free of suspicion – gave him delight. But now, he decided, was not the moment to build on it. First he must get her back to Sheffney House and into Gertie's care.

Signalling to Adam Kerby who waited with the phaeton further down the street, he told her, 'I'll drive you back to Sheffney House while my groom escorts your maid. As it happens, I am just come from calling on Gertie.' Calling in hope of seeing Elaine and disappointed not to have done so, he could admit to himself now.

Close as they were to the house, Elaine was glad to accept his offer. Once seated in the phaeton she used the short time she had to make some improvement to her appearance, pushing back her hair from her face and rescuing her bonnet. She was still engaged in unknotting the ribbons when Cato brought the vehicle to a halt. He did not immediately leap out of the vehicle and when she looked up to see why, she found him again regarding her intently.

'I meant what I said. Can you forget and forgive the mistakes of the past and allow us to make a new beginning? Will you trust me? Keep in view the possibility of our becoming friends?'

He looked and sounded more profoundly serious than she had ever known him to be. Feeling ridiculously shy, she returned her gaze to the bonnet and not trusting herself to speak, simply nodded.

'A promise?'

'Yes,' she managed.

Faint as it was, the word sang in his ears. 'Good!' he said, and with lithe ease, was out of the phaeton in a moment and round to hold up a hand to help her down from it. When she stood on the pavement he did not immediately release the hand he held but stood looking down at it. Then, very quietly, he said, 'I have always *meant* to be your friend. Blame my clumsiness for those offences you are going to forget and if I am clumsy again remember that I—' He wanted, quite desperately, to say 'I love you' but standing in the square in the middle of a grey day, both of them stained and dusty, was too antidotal to romance. And too soon – or so a diffidence entirely new to him made him believe. He substituted, '. . . that I do not mean to be.' Tame and unconvincing, he thought, but carrying her hand to his lips, gloveless and grimy as it was, he pressed a warm kiss on it.

He saw her into the house, stayed just long enough to explain Elaine's dishevelled state to Gertie and sing her fervent praises while Elaine herself slipped upstairs to wash and change.

Once more she found herself trying to unravel a tangle of emotions. How could she be so changeable? Be so *ready* to change? She had mistrusted Cato Raffen from their first meeting in John Woolford's book-room. Now she queried why. The details of that meeting were far less clear in her mind than they had been.

161

She had some memory of how she had *felt* at the time, but was less sure of the rest. She had thought he laughed at her. But had he? She had been in a poor state of health, had been nervous and shaken. Had that coloured her impression of him, created a prejudice that had distorted everything that had happened between them since? Or were her own wishes now looking to excuse him? Was she in fact ready to shrug off all caution because though he had asked for friendship, more had been implied?

Her only positive conclusion was that loving was a painful state of being hung on a pendulum swinging between hope and despondency. . . .

As though Fortune, in its arbitrary way, had suddenly decided to smile on him, Cato found himself with more time in which to pursue what he now acknowledged to himself was his courtship of Elaine.

It came about because on 22nd August, the Prince Regent retired to Brighton, worn out with playing host to so many often impertinent and graceless guests, to which was attached as always, the task of trying to please an obdurately ungrateful nation. The benefit to Cato was that for the present, the Regent would be making no public appearances in London. He was now able to be more frequently in the company of the ladies of Sheffney House and available to escort them to concert or party or to arrange a river trip to Richmond or Gravesend.

Gertie observed the increasing pleasure with which his presence was welcomed by Elaine with quizzical interest and wondered how long this flower among truces could keep its bloom. When given the opportunity of a tête-à-tête with Cato, she said teasingly, 'We see you with such gratifying frequency these days, Cato, it will not be long before I shall feel it my duty to ask you what your intentions are.'

'I think you know very well what they are,' he threw back at her.

'Yet it does not seem so long ago you thought you had no chance with her whose name we are not mentioning.'

'It was true at the time.'

'And now you think otherwise. When do you mean to put it to the test?'

'Not yet. I still have ground to make up.'

'And the Regent is abandoned to his fate? Or is the danger to him at an end?'

'No. But it is temporarily suspended. While he is in Brighton he is safe. *There* His Highness lives the life of a private gentleman. He comes and goes as he pleases with little notice to anyone. That offers small chance for my man to plan. And plan he does, carefully and intelligently. He does not mean to sacrifice his life needlessly. He proposes to escape the consequences of whatever action he takes and for that the way and the means must be set in place before the event. And so they are. Not to begin from Brighton, but from here in London. Little by little, I am getting closer to him, Gertie. He knows it . . . knows who I am. It rubs me raw to find him still ahead of me and time so short. It has become a duel between us – a duel I have to win.'

The lines of his face had tightened and hardened as he spoke and his eyes burned with a brightness Gertie remembered from earlier years when he was determined to achieve some aim. Even as a boy, he had not been able to endure failure in anything he undertook, the cost to his pride and his spirit too great. It appeared it was as much an essential part of him now, as it ever had been.

'How can you know so much and *not* know who he is?' she asked.

Impossible to explain how each discovery, however small, contributed something to defining the man. But circumstances had to be exactly right for that to offer a name. He had begun his search in the frustrating fog of the Regent's chivalrous refusal to disclose the name of the woman who had passed the warning to him. But a prince can never be wholly private and when Braxted had narrowed the choice for him he had discovered from which of those the warning had come and who it was had passed it to her. She had been reluctant to say and with good reason. Careful though he had been in his redirected enquiries, they had led to the attack on himself, an attack made by the groom's brother to protect himself and those with whom he worked. Their link to the principal mover of events was incidental, but it had provided a positive direction in which to look for his man.

He shrugged and answered Gertie's question as adequately as he could. 'In the beginning there was a group of plotters, its existence known to one or two who did not belong to it. But circumstances changed and the plotters scattered, their names blown away on the wind. That should have been the end of it had not one man taken fire from the idea and been prepared to carry it through. One man acting alone, single-minded, clever, courageous – and fanatical. He will make one more supreme effort to achieve his aim, I am certain.'

'But when? Where?'

'There is to be a last review in Hyde Park of men late returning from the Peninsula because of wounds and the like. In its way, it will be one more tribute to Wellington, and for that, esteeming the duke as he does, the Regent will come back to London. It will, I think, be an occasion of grave danger for him.'

'And you have the impossible task of saving the Regent from his own foolishness in not surrounding himself with guards!'

'I hope not to be quite alone in that, Gertie.' He gave her his wry smile. 'My hope is that Braxted will return in time to arrange that the Regent will be provided with more guards than he is aware of.'

164

His gaze sharpened. 'And speaking of Braxted— You know him better than I do, Gertie. Is he just amusing himself, or is he honestly looking to make Miss Marney his marchioness?'

'What James looks to do, I cannot say,' Gertie said crossly. 'As I have said before, of all men, I should not expect him to marry except into a family at least equal in rank to his own. But he has given me no hint.'

Cato's smile took on a steely quality. 'You need have no doubt now, that I mean to marry her if she'll have me. And if that runs counter to anything Braxted has in mind, so be it!'

In pursuit of that intention he continued his attentions to Elaine until it was impossible for her to mistake that she was being courted as she never had been before, quietly, subtly and with a great deal of charm, by a man generously committed to proving himself in love. The world seemed to change about her: happiness made her vaguely light-headed. Now she found herself looking for and admiring the very traits in him that she had most frowned on in the past, particularly his readiness to meet the vagaries of life with laughter. And a certain expression in his eyes when he looked at her woke a warmth and excitement in her she had never experienced before.

Happiness lent courage to her confidence. The water-lily box again swam above its reflection in the polished wood of her chest-of-drawers. . . .

Preoccupied with what seemed to be the realization of a dream, the increasing frequency of Oliver's civilities passed Elaine by. She accepted the flowers, the letters, the outings with a kind of dutiful resignation in accordance with what she knew Gertie thought of as the least part of what was 'due to the family'. She woke from her abstraction when Oliver, having driven her in a

165

hired chaise to Hampstead, treated her to an elegant lunch at a pleasant inn, walked with her on the Heath and there proposed to her.

With a lurch of the heart, she leapt into awareness of how foolish she had been not to have been prepared for this.

Listening to her carefully phrased refusal with mounting anger, Oliver was sorely tempted to tell her how small was his interest in her person, that she was to him no more than a stepping-stone to Sarah's fortune. Swallowing his gall however, he begged her to believe how much he loved and admired her . . . begged her not to allow this to be her final answer but to give thought to all the advantages of their marrying.

Recognizing the reluctance with which Oliver gave up an idea once thought of, Elaine agreed, foolish though she knew it to be. They walked the short distance back to the inn where the chaise waited for them, each busy with their own thoughts. Elaine had time to reflect that while the advantage to Oliver of their marrying was easily seen, his conceit must have extraordinary range if he thought she could perceive any accruing to herself from it.

Oliver restrained his impatience with difficulty. If the damned female did not change her mind – and soon – he would be facing difficulties from which he would find it hard to escape. He had done his best to charm and not succeeded. Sarah's fortune was no longer simply a desirable goal: possession of it had become a necessity, his best means of preservation from several unhappy possibilities. He needed to make alternative plans.

His thoughts turned to ways of forcing a reluctant woman into marriage. The extreme of those was rape: used through the centuries by more than a few determined men hungry for what an heiress owned or represented. In his own case, though, there was a further option available, quicker and more certain than marriage . . . *murder*. He did not shrink from the thought. He had had close dealings with several groups of smugglers in past

166

years and learned from them not to be squeamish when self-interest was involved.

He made no firm decision, but allowed the thoughts to lie in the shadowed margins of his mind to await events. . . .

CHAPTER FIFTEEN

September began with a week of showery weather followed by
two days of high winds before settling to the seasonal expectation of misty mornings and gentle sunshine.

No more news had been received of Lord Sheffney's coming
and Gertie was growing discontented again but still had no intention of leaving London before her lord's return. However, Fanny,
now in better health, came with John to spend a few days and
lighten her sister's mood. And as London society grew thin, there
was leisure to read and re-read the year's literary pleasures which
included another novel, *Mansfield Park*, from the pen of the
author of *Pride and Prejudice*, two long narrative poems from
Byron, and an anonymously published historical novel, *Waverley,*
that had created a furore and provoked wild guesses as to its
author.

Attending a musical evening given by the Bouveries, Gertie left
her seat during an interval to speak to Lady Castlereagh and, a
moment or two later, Elaine found Léon Dacier standing beside
her. His hand on the back of the vacant chair, he asked, 'You
permit, *mademoiselle?*'

Elaine gave smiling assent and, sitting down, the lieutenant
said, 'You still do not remove into the country?'

169

'No. The countess has no thought of going before her husband returns from Paris.' She gave him an interested glance. 'And you, *m'sieur*? We are flattered that you still remain in England when so many of your countrymen could not wait to leave us.'

He shrugged good-humouredly. 'There were few of us who were your willing guests, *mam'selle*. My good fortune was to have both funds and family connections in this country. They make my – my residence here more *agréable*. But my heart belongs to France as much as do those of my compatriots and I, too, go soon. It is what I come to tell you.'

'You have many friends here. We shall all be sorry to lose you, yet would not wish to keep you from where you very naturally want to be.'

There was a pause before he spoke again, then softly but with emphasis, he said, 'Some part of my heart I leave in England. There are those I shall regret not to see. One most *particulière-ment*.'

The words were accompanied by so earnest a look that Elaine could not doubt they were meant for her. Her colour rose but she said only, 'I am sorry the reason for your being here was not a happier one, but I shall never forget how much I owe to one particular Frenchman.'

'It was my privilege to be of service. If it makes you remember me with kindness I shall be glad.'

'Indeed I shall! Perhaps one day we shall meet again now that our countries are no longer at war. That is something we both may be thankful for.'

That struck a spark that flared momentarily in his dark eyes. 'You will permit me to wish that it had ended differently, though. You have the nature *sympathique* and to you I may speak of my desolation that my country's leader . . . that Napoleon Bonaparte, whose greatness many of your own countrymen recognize, is brought low. And now his army – *my* army – is to be officered by the *émigrés*, who were our enemies!'

It was natural that he should feel so – and feel it strongly – Elaine reminded herself, but she was not one of Napoleon's English admirers and could offer no agreement on this point. Before she had thought of anything she could safely say, Dacier glanced past her and stood up.

'Madam the Countess returns. I make some part of my adieux to you both now, but hope to wait on you at Sheffney House to do so how you say? – in form.'

He gazed down at her, his look warm yet sombre. 'To you, Miss Marney, I say goodbye with much regret. I do not know what waits for me in France. I wish I—' He broke off with a shake of his head. 'It does not signify, though I ask again for you to keep some kindness in your heart for me.'

Oliver had never heard of Nemesis, but he felt the goddess's cold, avenging shadow stretching towards him as the days slipped by. Having completed the business that had brought him back again to London, he had kicked his heels in town too long in hope of yet persuading Cousin Elaine into matrimony. The consequences promised disaster because, in the intervals between dancing attention on the damnable bitch, he had been so bored he had indulged his taste for expensive pleasures, unable to relinquish the idea that they would soon be commonplace in his style of living.

Gambling was the darling sin of the age and with what he thought was no more than a right and proper confidence in his power of play, he had been drawn to pass a number of evenings in two of the lesser gambling houses existing outside the golden square mile of the *beau monde*. He had won: he had lost. But whereas his winning had been of short duration, his losing had continued. Now, when his leaving London was fixed and immutable, he was in desperate need of recovering his losses. In the cold light of day, he could not fool himself that faithfully as he had performed the chief part of the business that had brought him to London, his partners in the transaction would overlook the least shortfall in what they were due.

He had no lack of animal courage, or he would never have thrown in his lot as far as he had with the smuggling fraternity. It was to dice with the devil, but the rewards were high and he could foresee no reason why he should fall foul of them. Later, witnessing some of the appalling punishments inflicted on those who *did*, his determination to avoid drawing like reprisals on himself had been notably strengthened.

Cash in advance had been the condition on which the present joint enterprise was to be undertaken and he at the London end of it had been negotiator and stake-holder. The risks of the whole undertaking being exceptional, the price demanded matched. He could think now, that when the luck had turned against him, only some disorder of the mind could have made him suspend caution and be led on to borrow from the sum he held on his confederates' behalf. The sudden, chilling recollection of how little time was left to him before the consequences of deficit had to be faced brought him up short. A night of desperate thought produced only one possible hope of deliverance and took him to Sheffney House the next day.

Luck now made him a small amend; Gertie was closeted with her *modiste* when he arrived in the late morning and he had Elaine to himself.

Elaine received news of his arrival with dismay. After declining his offer of marriage, she had hoped for more respite from his attentions than she had been given.

A first glance at Oliver standing in the clear light of a fine mid-September day falling through the one tall window of the Primrose Parlour, showed Elaine that Oliver was in a disturbed state of mind. His neckcloth was tied awry and his waistcoat was of the gaudier kind he usually avoided when calling at Sheffney House.

Oliver had thought he could present his petition in easy style, but after a brief exchange of greetings he found himself floundering through a series of unfinished sentences. He blamed Elaine's cool unrevealing expression for that and fell into silence. For a moment he sat staring at the carpet, hearing her speak but not taking in the words. Then, with an exclamation, he sprang to his feet, cutting across what she was saying with, 'Cousin, I'm forced to appeal to your generosity! I'm in a damnable fix. I've been a fool . . . lost money at cards I cannot afford . . . do not have. A debt of honour that must be paid. And soon!' That hadn't sounded too bad, he thought, and ended, 'I need a loan . . . must throw myself on your mercy.'

Elaine's first reaction was relief that this wasn't another proposal. It was followed by surprise. The blow to Oliver's pride caused by having to make such an application must be considerable. She looked at him wonderingly. 'How much do you need?'

'Five hundred pounds.'

The sum astonished her. 'I have nothing like that sum at hand. Nor can I come by so much before next quarter day at the end of the month.'

Oliver, on a knife-edge of need and nerves, parted with a little more of his restraint. 'You don't understand! I *must* have it! You're my only hope. Matters are worse than I have yet told you. My life is threatened! Cannot you get it from that lawyer fellow, Woolford? Or ask the woman you're living with? He flung out his hands expressively. 'God! She must be rolling in riches.'

There was genuine fear behind his words, a feverish passion of anxiety, Elaine heard it in his voice, saw it in the darkening of his ruddy colouring. Something graver than an unpaid gaming debt must surely be involved. . . . Beyond knowing he owned a carrier's business, she knew little about his circumstances and she wondered whether such a simple, commonplace line of commerce could be dubiously used.

'I will do what I can, Oliver,' she said uncomfortably. 'But it will not be easy to raise even half as much.'

'I can wait three days. The third day from today, say. Cannot you have it by then?' He stared at her, every sense at full stretch to compel her to meet his need. 'Two days after that I have to leave London.'

'I'll do my best, Oliver. Find as much as I can. I cannot promise more.'

The visible surge of relief she saw in his expression made her wonder if he had taken in the modification of her promise.

Grasping at the promise of relief, Oliver did not quibble over shades of difference. He had asked for more than he needed. Somehow she would – *must* – find him enough. Wasting no time on polite nothings, he bade her goodbye, leaving her with the last minute, vehement injunction, '*Don't fail me, Cousin.*'

By contrast with the uneasiness Oliver's morning importunity aroused in her, the evening promised only pleasure for Elaine.

Though the season was indisputably at an end, Lady Mary Lawrens was giving a ball to which Gertie, Elaine and Cato were all to go.

Young, vivacious, fun-loving Lady Lawrens had recently presented her husband with a fine, healthy heir, but in the process of doing so she had been forced to forego the season's delights in this year of all years. The reward she claimed was to spend a few weeks in London in which to enjoy whatever the capital still had to offer. Her husband was pleased to indulge her, but because it was not worth opening their town house for so short a time, they were ensconced at Grillons. Rooms at White's Club were hired for the ball and every provision made to attract

as many as possible of their friends and acquaintance still lingering in town.

Cato had sent word to Gertie that though affairs made him
uncertain of being able to escort them to the ball, he hoped to
have that pleasure on their return from it.

Elaine was looking forward to the occasion with an inner
excitement, an expectancy, she could not entirely explain. In the
past weeks she had been conscious that Cato was behaving
impeccably towards her. Not once had he attempted to kiss her,
though she had sensed that at times he had found it hard to
restrain himself from doing so. Perversely, she was now ready to
welcome what he withheld. She no longer doubted that he loved
her and was even more certain that she loved him. Remembering
the many sharp reversals of their acquaintance, she could not
help but wonder at it. It was as though love – subversive and inde-
pendent – had not needed her consciousness of it to exist.

Gertie watched the progress of this late wooing and reflected
with a degree of whimsical resignation on the *unexpectedness* of
Elaine's path towards marriage. Co-operative and conformable
though the girl had been – except for that one extraordinary lapse
that had taken her to Hyde Park alone – nothing had gone as
she, Gertie, had anticipated. And that in the end it should be
Cato. . . . Much as she liked Elaine, she had found it a little difficult to relinquish the idea of a brilliant marriage for him. And
what of James? If against all odds, he pre-empted Cato's intention to propose to Elaine, did Elaine care enough for Cato to
resist such a glittering prize?

There was sufficient a squeeze at White's when Gertie and
Elaine arrived to promise the Lawrenses their ball would be a
success. There was even a slightly feverish atmosphere among
the guests as though they were determined to wring all possible
enjoyment from what must surely be the last ball of any importance this year. Allowing herself to appear to be swept along with

175

the brittle mood of the evening, Elaine did her best to pay civil attention to her company while watching impatiently for Cato's arrival. For all that she missed it when it happened.

Cato's seeking gaze found her at once. She was talking to two attentive gentlemen and it seemed to him that, glowing and lovely, she stood out from all the other women in the room.

Her gown was of a rich apricot *charmeuse* with a deep band of silver bugle embroidery at the hem and decorating the minute puffed sleeves. A band of apricot velvet was woven through her hair and caught at the sides with twin clasps of brilliants. Completing the picture, she carried an elegant fan of white feathers. Now that his defences were down, he freely acknowledged that he was besotted, helplessly in thrall without any wish to escape. He wanted her, needed her, could not bear the thought that she might prefer any other man to himself. Gazing at her across the distance, he wondered if the first link in the chains that bound him had been forged when he looked down at her unconscious face at The Griffin. He had no answer to that and it did not matter.

Taken by surprise when he came to her side, Elaine was off guard and her delight in seeing him shone out unmistakably. Cato bowed, murmured a conventional greeting, but could hardly contain his jubilation. That revealing look sent his spirits soaring. He thought triumphantly, She's mine! I'll speak to her tonight. . . .

He was given no early opportunity. In the short time that remained before the supper interval Elaine, now in sparkling form, was either dancing or surrounded and when the general drift towards the waiting tables began she was one of a largish party. Managing to reach her side, he grasped her elbow and whispered, 'I *must* speak to you. Privately. Make time for me after supper, I beg.'

She turned to look at him and read in the warmth and urgency

176

of his expression enough to guess what he was intending to say. Her heart sang and an almost suffocating joy flooded her but she could do no more than nod agreement before she was swept on by those surrounding her.

Briefly, Cato considered making a push to join them – Gertie would make space for him – but then he saw that the Marquis of Braxted was back in town and was now walking beside Elaine, had taken her hand on his arm, and he decided against it.

Let the noble lord have his moment. What could he achieve in the course of a supper-hour?

CHAPTER SIXTEEN

hen supper was over, the Marquis of Braxted was again Elaine's escort. In the ballroom, when she would have removed her hand from his arm, he locked it into place with his free hand and when she looked her surprise, he said, 'Come with me. There is something I want to show you.'

He led her away from their immediate company into a passage revealing several closed doors, one of which he opened to usher her into a small candle-lit sitting-room. A central table had two or three chairs set round it, and other, more comfortable chairs flanked a cheerful little fire.

Observing the conventions, he closed-to the door without engaging the lock before leading her further into the room and then stood gazing at her again with smiling brightness.

Impatient to be free to go in search of Cato, Elaine cast a quick glance about the room seeking the special object Braxted was to show her. Nothing in its small confine appeared of particular interest and she looked back at him with an enquiring lift of her brows.

For once, it seemed, James Valdoe, darkly handsome and fastidiously elegant as ever, was bereft of his usual suavity. At last, with an effort, he said, 'I must ask your pardon, Miss Marney. I have nothing to show you, but there is something I want – *need* to tell you. It is of great importance to me but I cannot cannot guess how you will receive it.'

Thoroughly puzzled, Elaine could think of no subject the marquis might put forward that could induce such obvious hesitancy. A proposal? An offer of a different nature? She would be surprised to receive either, but she was certain this worldly-wise man would have no difficulty presenting either, with ease and charm, if he so chose.

'I have just this day returned from Dorset,' he said after a pause, 'and by one means and another I have established the truth of what I have to tell you beyond all doubt. Unsuitable as the occasion is, I find myself unable to wait for a better. My fear is that what delights me may be less than pleasing to you.'

More puzzled than ever, Elaine could only wait for him to continue.

'I told you some weeks ago that Joseph Marney was once my tutor. Had we not been interrupted, I would have told you more – would have told you I also knew your mother.' He gave a quick, searching glance and went on quickly, 'It is an old story and no uncommon one. We fell in love. I was twenty, Marianne was seventeen. Even though she was of good family – her father a Roding and rector of Cheveney Cresset, a nearby village – she was of insufficient consequence for my father to agree to our marrying. I was too well acquainted with his pride even to suggest it to him. But I had only a year to wait for my majority and though it had been arranged for some time that I should accompany my cousin on a two-year tour of Italy and where else was possible at that time, I promised myself I would return the day after my twenty-first birthday to marry my love. We were to go under the escort of my cousin's tutor, my father finding it more convenient to retain mine in the place of his secretary who was about to retire.'

He paused again, stood looking inward, frowning on memory

before continuing harshly, 'Like any young fool, I made the mistake of bidding her farewell in a secluded place on the eve of my departure. Hot-blooded, irresponsible, on a crest of emotion, I seduced her, believing I was taking sufficient precautions against any consequences. Marianne was wholly innocent and I in my ignorance and arrogance left her pregnant.'

Watching him with concern, Elaine began to suspect to what end the story was leading but was too astonished to know what she felt about it.

Still looking back bleakly across the years, Braxted continued, 'Every care was taken to prevent my knowing it. I returned as I had intended as soon as I was of age. I found Marianne had married three months after I left England and that she and her husband had immediately left the neighbourhood. She had married Joseph Marney. Not unattractive in his person but more than twenty years her age and a cold, clever, humourless man. The tale told me was that he had proposed to her on the strength of an unexpected legacy of a thousand pounds with which he intended to start a school. That was something I knew he had long wanted to do and so I believed what they said. Everyone told the same tale . . . the marriage had come about as result of the legacy. For the daughter of a country rector estranged from his family, it could be thought an acceptable match.

'Never guessing the reason, I was young enough for my pride to be outraged that Marianne had not waited for me, but knowing her nature to be gentle and yielding, I had just enough generosity to suppose she had been swayed by those who wished her well to take the security offered. If she told anyone of the promise I had made her, I don't doubt they would have pointed out the notorious unreliability of promises made by young men in my position. But I burned with rage. I blamed Marianne for inconstancy. I blamed Joseph Marney simply for having married her. Not once did it occur to me that all the blame was mine.'

His tone dropped to a greater depth of bitterness. 'Had I used my intelligence in the way Marney himself had taught me, I would have suspected my father's hand in the matter. There was no legacy, of course. Faced with the rector's demand that I return from my travels to marry his daughter, my noble sire had refused outright, but to keep the matter from open scandal had bribed his secretary with a thousand pounds to marry the girl inconveniently impregnated by his son. The conditions made were that they should then both remove as far as possible from the locality, leaving no hint of their destination and under no circumstances to return. Those conditions were kept.' He brought his gaze back from distance, looked at her sombrely. 'The rest of the story is yours.'

Her voice husky with wonder, Elaine said slowly, 'What you are saying – what it amounts to is that I am your natural daughter?'

'Yes. Is the thought abhorrent to you?'

Elaine shook her head. 'But it is hard to take in . . . to adjust. What I don't understand is what, after so many years, first made you think it possible?'

'It was when you told me your second name – *Luce*. That supported by the information that you were a little older than I thought. Luce is one of *my* names. It is the one Marianne always used when we were alone. Joseph Marney cannot have known the name was mine. If he had, he would never have tolerated it being given to you, I am certain. A brilliant scholar, a good teacher, but a man devoid of warmth. When I think of the pressures that must have been put on your mother to marry him . . . of the unhappiness that must have followed—' He left the sentence unfinished.

Looking back, Elaine suspected that it was true that her mother had known little happiness in her marriage. She could not recollect the man she had thought to be her father ever showing any warmth of feeling to the child that bore his name. But within his

182

limitations, Joseph Marney had been fair in his dealings with her, giving due approval for application to learning and to achievement. She had learned early to expect no more.

'There is a great deal we need to talk about, but I have already kept you here longer than I should. For my peace of mind, tell me— Before tonight I think you have had some liking for me?'

She gave him a wavering smile. 'And still have.'

'Then I shall hope to improve on that for I have the greatest pleasure in finding I have a daughter like you.' He stepped nearer to her, put his hands on her shoulders and gazed down with the first glimmer of a smile turning his lips. 'You are the living image of your mother, but otherwise are so very much yourself. I should like to think, though, that somewhere in you there is one small virtue that I may claim to be my gift to you.'

Cato looked for Elaine after supper with growing impatience. Gertie was unable to tell him where she was, but Lady Jersey who was talking to the countess, was able to supply a general direction. Never averse to setting a cat among the pigeons, she forbore to mention Elaine had not left the room alone.

The passage Cato entered had a dead end but one door was slightly ajar showing an edge of candlelight. He pushed it open a cautious inch or two not wanting to intrude upon anyone seeking privacy. The small gap revealed a tableau of two people entirely engrossed in each other. Braxted's hands were clasped on Elaine's shoulders and as Cato watched, he drew her into a close embrace. His words and the warmth with which he spoke, though spoken softly, carried clearly to Cato. 'Remember from now forward you are under my protection.' He put his lips to her brow then as though setting a seal on his pledge.

The interpretation of Braxted's words could not be mistaken: it was the common phrase that expressed a man's willingness to shelter and provide for a woman who consented to be his mistress.

Pulling the door to, Cato turned and walked back the way he had come.

It was a full half an hour after supper had ended before Braxted brought Elaine to Gertie's side. When His Lordship left them, the countess turned an unsmiling face to Elaine to ask with unusual sharpness, 'Where have you been? Did you see Cato?'

Answering only the second question, Elaine said, 'No. But I must look for him now. He said he wished to speak to me.'

'You won't find him. He's gone. He was in one of his rare, quiet rages. I thought you might have met and quarrelled. He would not discuss it and if it was not to do with you, I have no clue to what was the cause.'

'Am I the only person he quarrels with?' The question hovered between amusement and annoyance. Briefly Elaine wondered if he had been vexed because she had kept him waiting. How long had she been with Braxted? Possibly longer than she had realized. But she could not believe that Cato would have left in a sulk. There must have been some other, some more forceful reason. She comforted herself with the assurance that he would call at Sheffney House next day and explain. What *she* could not yet tell Gertie was what had passed between herself and Braxted.

Braxted had said, 'Let what I have told you remain a secret between us a little longer. There are ramifications that need careful consideration. You were born after the marriage between Marney and Marianne. Legally and in the eyes of the world, you are a child of that marriage. If *I* were married I could adopt you. As it is, I must think of what is most in your interest.' And there it had been left.

Cato came next day as Elaine had hopefully anticipated – but not with explanations.

Elaine was in the Primrose Parlour when he walked in. Putting down her sewing, she rose on a surge of relief, turning a smiling face towards him. Relief and smile both faded when she saw the coldness with which he looked at her. His bow was perfunctory and standing a few steps inside the door, he made no attempt to come nearer to her.

Attempting normality, she offered, 'Won't you come in and sit down? Gertie will be back soon.'

He inclined his head but made no move towards a chair. A little desperately, Elaine said, 'You left the Lawrenses' ball unexpectedly early.'

His mouth twisted into a small, cynical smile. 'For an unexpected reason.'

The look, the tone, implied that she had supplied the reason. 'If I kept you waiting, I apologize. I was—' She hesitated.

'Unavoidably detained,' he finished for her in a tone of contempt.

'I cannot think why you sound so cross. I thought we had reached a happier understanding.'

'I thought so, too. But I think now I have never truly understood you. One of those mistakes by which we learn. Painfully.' He shrugged. 'However, everything passes.'

His hostility was too deliberate not to be recognized. He appeared to have come simply to demonstrate it. Pain twisted like a knife in her. Shocked, bewildered, she stared at him without speaking until pride woke and prodded her into speech and into matching his coolness. 'Indeed! It happens to us all. It is too easy to mistake shadow for substance.'

But she felt too physically sick to remain in the room with him.

185

As she walked to the door, she said, 'Pray excuse me. Newbald will have told Gertie you are here.'

He bowed, held the door wide for her, his expression wooden.

Leaden-footed, Elaine climbed the stairs towards her room. She had believed there could never again be deep division between them, that the days of misunderstandings were past. Through a blur of tears, she saw Gertie cross the hall and enter the room she had just left.

Gertie's eyebrows signalled her surprise at finding Cato alone: Newbald had told her Miss Marney was with him. But there was something in the air . . . Cato was looking mulish. Leaping to the right conclusion, she said, 'Heaven give me patience! Don't tell me you and Elaine have quarrelled again! Cannot you be together for five minutes without falling into dispute?'

'It seems not.'

The carelessly spoken words and accompanying shrug did not deceive Gertie: his mood had abated nothing from when she had last seen him. So it *did* have to do with Elaine. . . . Yet Elaine had appeared to be genuinely at a loss as to the reason.

'Finding we had nothing comfortable to say to each other, very sensibly Miss Marney left me to amuse myself,' Cato told her waspishly.

'But what has *happened* between you? Have you offered and been turned down?'

'No. Fortunately I was saved from making such a fool of myself.'

'*Cato*! It was not long ago you told me she was the only woman for you!'

'I was mistaken. Miss Marney is not the woman I thought her.'

'How can that be! What *can* you have quarrelled about? You must know she loves you, Cato. Even I am certain of it now.'

'And I have not a doubt you will find yourself as mistaken in that as I was.'

186

He was bitterly angry, Gertie saw, but there was nothing she could do for him unless he confided in her. It was clear he did not mean to do so and a little tartly, she told him, 'Without knowing what has happened between you, I can say nothing useful.'

'Nothing useful or otherwise, *can* be said. The thing is at an end.'

Stony-faced, he then declared himself to be in haste to be else-where and Gertie made no attempt to press him to stay.

Following that visit, Elaine retreated into silent, white-faced misery that prohibited questions. But it was misery barbed with anger. She could think of nothing she had done to bring about such a reversal of her happiness. The wonder of what Braxted had told her was lost, submerged by it.

On the third day after the Lawrenses' ball, Elaine was in her bedroom trying to concentrate on sorting silks for a new embroi-dery. She was having little success. Her thoughts kept slipping away into a grey limbo of unhappiness that left her staring into space, seeing nothing, her mind a daze of memories of laughter shared with Cato Raffen, of the quiet joy she had known in the past weeks . . . memories now made worthless and cruel in their remembering.

Polly Cutts, coming in to tell her that Mr Marney had just been shown into the drawing-room shocked her into the realization she had utterly forgotten her promise to Oliver.

Oliver had been pacing the floor of the long, elegant drawing-room, the evidence of wealth wherever he looked an added provocation to his renewed quake and fury at the situation in which he found himself. He swung to the door as Elaine entered, so fierce an intensity of expectation in his face that Elaine longed to retreat. Instead, she rushed into nervous speech.

'Oliver! I'm so sorry. I forgot— So much has happened—'

'*Forgot!*' It was beyond Oliver's immediate acceptance that his desperate need could be forgotten. In a voice loud with disbelief, he said, 'You haven't got the money! *Any* of it?'

She shook her head. She had expected his anger, but not the look of murderous fury that blazed across his face. It launched her into speech again.

'I'll give you all I have . . . ask Gertie to lend me what she can, but I fear it will be nowhere near the sum you want.' He had no idea what it cost her to make the offer. It was not a favour she would have asked Gertie for on her own behalf, but she could see no other way of providing a worthwhile part of what Oliver needed.

Oliver stared speechlessly at her, his mind in turmoil. 'Wait!' he said imperatively and turning from her, marched over to one of the windows overlooking the square.

Unaccustomed to exercising restraint, it was with difficulty that he forced control on the fury that had made him want to strike her down. But he needed to *think*, to find something more dependable than maybe, perhaps, and small dole. He needed, above all, a sure and certain life-preserver. . . . And the best and surest provider of that would be possession of Great-aunt Sarah's fortune. *And soon!* With that in hand or very nearly, if he promised his smuggling partners twice what they were due, gave proof of its certainty, he could surely bring them to tolerate a small delay. The first essential then, was to remove the one obstacle standing between him and preservation – Cousin Elaine. Well timed to be of maximum use, there slithered into his mind the recollection that in a day or two he would have the means at hand by which it could be done – and he himself left with clean hands. . . .

On a surge of hope and relief he turned back to Elaine and forced his mouth to smile.

'Forgive me, Cousin Elaine. My nerves have been at stretch. If you will put together what you can and do it without mentioning my name to Her Ladyship, I should be grateful. You haven't mentioned it to her yet?'

Elaine shook her head, too relieved to question this sudden access of mildness.

'Good. A man doesn't like— Well, you may guess how it is.' He shrugged in a man-of-the-world fashion. 'Her Ladyship might not understand. But between cousins, what matter, eh? Once I am on home ground I can soon pay you back. I think I have let myself be over-impressed by things said. . . . A gambling debt has to be paid, however, and I now begin to see a way to raise some part of what I need and with your help shall no doubt contrive to find my way to the whole. A man can be mistaken in the character of those with whom he plays, but a lesson learned. . . .' He left it there with another shrug.

It was all too glib, but Elaine could not see that it mattered. To end this unpleasant meeting, she was ready to promise that he should have every penny she could scrape together and much as it went against the grain, she would even borrow from Gertie.

Oliver waved a hand towards the windows. 'Those gardens in the square . . . you could walk in them without needing a maid with you, surely?'

'Yes. Only the residents who have keys can get in. I have walked there alone a number of times.' The suggestion of secrecy added a little more to the slight uneasiness his glibness had aroused, but it was too slight really to trouble her.

'That makes it an easy matter for us to meet privately. The gate over to the left, looking out from here – meet me there prompt at eleven of the clock the day after tomorrow with whatever you have managed and we can settle the business comfortably away from interference. I'll be going out of town that same day.'

There was an eagerness and confidence about him about him now that was a long way from the mood in which he had first met her.

189

'Very well,' Elaine agreed. thankful to hear he had a definite date for departure. She felt she had been let off lightly and was cheered by it.

'You won't fail me again, will you. Cousin Elaine?' There was more force of command than of appeal in Oliver's voice.

'No,' Elaine said almost fervently. 'I won't.'

Only when the door had closed on him did the thought come to startle her, But I'm not his cousin! There is no relationship between us at all!

CHAPTER SEVENTEEN

*T*he review for which the Regent had returned from Brighton late the previous afternoon was to begin at eleven o'clock, the same hour at which Elaine was to meet Oliver. As on other occasions, His Royal Highness had refused either to cancel or defer the event in the interests of his own safety.

Cato began his surveillance in Hyde Park an hour earlier. Even with the need to give his entire attention to what he was doing, he found it difficult to block out the anger that had burned through his every thought from the time he had closed the door on Braxted and Elaine. He forced himself to do it though, because coolness of mind and quickness of perception were essential now or the whole undertaking had been for nothing. He had no doubt that the anger would remain, molten and inextinguishable, waiting to reassert its power.

Prowling through the crowd as it began to gather along the route of the march, every nerve was stretched to quivering capacity. Nothing had lessened his belief that today the Regent stood at greatest risk; that this was the assassin's last chance and something would – *must* – happen. It was a bitter blow to his pride that he had come to this crucial hour without being able to identify the man. Only his capture and delivery to justice with no harm done to the Regent could compensate for his feeling of falling short of competence. It was curious that he remained convinced that he would recognize the man when – and if – he saw him. His fear was that recognition might come too late. It was a formidable spur to his vigilance. That others besides himself were watching did nothing to diminish his acceptance of ultimate responsibility.

The public's appetite for the pomp of a parade appeared little less than it had been throughout the summer to judge by the steadily increasing crowd. Around the podium on which the Regent would stand, people were being marshalled into place more purposefully than usual and held behind ropes at a greater than usual distance. On the perimeter of the parade area those who came in carriages were finding places that would allow their occupants to sit in comfort with a clear view over the heads of those standing. The last to come were the younger, more active members of society who were prepared to stand on their feet to obtain the best view of all and who were permitted to take places inside the hempen barriers as though by indisputable right. The likelihood of danger from these easily identifiable scions of the privileged was considered too remote. For all that, Cato scrutinized each group as it formed.

Miss Pilford was the centre of one such. For a few moments he allowed himself the pleasure of watching her. Talking and laughing in her lively way, she was as pretty as ever in a delicate white muslin gown trimmed with jade-green ribbons, a fetching bonnet to match and a perky parasol. The friends round her included Jeremy Lazelle, obviously off duty, two other young women and their escorts, all known to Cato, at least by sight. Not a group likely to embrace someone who harboured the dark ambition to remove the Regent from this world. Yet it was these few isolated groups which were best placed to bring a marksman within pistol-shot of the Regent. His gaze passed on to the next group.

The Prince's well-guarded cortège arrived on time. With something like resignation, Cato watched the substantial figure step down from the carriage and up on to the podium. Magnificently encased in a uniform glittering with silver lace, gold bullion and bright buttons, the Regent offered a generous target to even a mediocre marksman.

Somewhere out of sight, fife and drum had begun a lively tune and in a short time the first of the marchers came into sight. With its usual mindless partiality, the crowd happily booed the Prince and cheered the troops, the sounds mingled and inextricable. Here and there were small eddies of movement as people came and went. Harmless in themselves, they made an extra hazard because they drew the eye and could do so at what might prove a critical moment.

Cato's gaze slid anxiously back and forth over those nearest to the Prince, his tension growing as the marching ranks went by. Nothing. . . . And again, nothing. . . . Yet his certainty that the assassin was here grew as though his presence could be felt at his nerve ends.

His glance skimmed Miss Pilford's group, paused, moved on, swept back. There was change. It was larger by one. The newcomer was Lieutenant Dacier. A Frenchman. That he had expected. A Frenchman in no hurry to return to his country. . . . But Dacier, prominent in society and with English connections?

At this moment, Dacier's head was bent towards Miss Pilford as though engrossed in what she was saying. *But his intent gaze was fixed on the Regent and his right hand was in the pocket of his riding coat. . . .*

Elaine stood just inside the gate of the gardens that Oliver had appointed as their meeting place. She had come early, as though by doing so she could hurry on the disagreeable transaction.

Asking Gertie for a loan had been as distasteful as she had expected and she had stumbled awkwardly through the business unable to offer a clear reason for wanting the money.

To the hundred pounds Gertie had lent her she had added forty pounds of her own money, which was all she had remaining to her of her quarterly allowance but which left the total considerably short of what Oliver had originally asked for. The quicksilver change Oliver had undergone during that last meeting nagged at her now, but her only conclusion was that she should be thankful for it. As a distant clock struck eleven she found herself praying he would not be late. There was something about the surreptitious nature of this meeting that made her uneasy, as though through it, some taint of whatever shabby dealing Oliver was involved in rubbed off on her.

The last stroke of the hour had barely sounded however, when a dusty carriage and pair rattled to a halt outside the gate and Oliver thrust his head out of its window. When Elaine showed herself at the gate, he beckoned to her, saying, 'Come. Get in. We can conduct our business more comfortably here.' He opened the carriage door.

It seemed an excess of caution to Elaine, but it was not worth disputing and grasping the hand Oliver held out to her, she stepped up into the vehicle.

Sitting down beside him, she handed him the bag of money she was carrying, saying, 'A hundred and forty pounds, Oliver. It is all I could manage in the time.'

He weighed the bag in his hand as though it was of small interest to him before sliding it into a pocket. His brilliant blue eyes flicked a swift, probing look at her. 'And no one knows you are here?'

'No.'

His smile grew as he looked at her. 'Then thank you, dear Cousin.'

The mockery in his tone was loud and clear and even as he spoke, he reached up and rapped sharply on the panel behind the coachman's bench. At once the carriage was on the move and within moments the horses had reached a smart trot.

The alarm with which she looked at him broadened Oliver's smile to a grin of triumph. 'We're taking a little ride, as we have done on other occasions,' he told her.

But with an unmistakable difference this time, instinct warned her.

'No!' Elaine declared, and reached for the nearer door handle. Instantly, Oliver's powerful hand clamped down on hers, crushing it painfully.

'So eager to leave me? I shan't allow it, you know. Just sit quiet and enjoy the jaunt while you can.' And then, when Elaine drew a deeper breath, added, 'Scream if you wish, my dear, the coachman'll hear nothing he's not paid to hear. But if your din annoys me, I'll pour enough laudanum into you, to keep you quiet a long time. A *very* long time.' He drew a small phial out of a pocket as he spoke and showed it to her.

She had no doubt at all that he meant what he said. Whatever it was he wanted from her, he meant to have. Not only meant to have, but was confident of getting. There was a quivering excitement in him, an anticipation of success. Escape from whatever it was he planned for her must wait upon chance, even if all that offered was to throw herself out of the carriage at the risk of injury.

As though he read her thoughts, Oliver pulled her left arm through his right and grappled it to his side. 'In less than half an hour we'll be there,' he assured her with smug satisfaction.

'Where?' Elaine moistened dry lips.

'You'll see soon enough.'

He had asked for secrecy and, unthinkingly, she had complied. No one knew where she was, what she was doing, who she was with. If her mind had been less dulled by the wretchedness Cato Raffen had inflicted on her, she might have questioned Oliver's reasons. But she hadn't and it was useless to waste lamentations on it now.

195

She turned her attention to the streets through which they were passing in an attempt to recognize their route. She had an impression it ran south and east, but could not be certain. Already they had passed out of localities with which she had become familiar and into meaner streets. Before long, on her right, she began to glimpse masts and derricks at the end of short, narrow alleys, indicating they were near the Thames, suggesting she was right about the direction.

Though lapped in complacency, Oliver's hold on her arm did not slacken and even when the narrowness of the streets forced the coachman to let the horses' pace drop to a walk she was given no opportunity to throw herself out of the carriage. Growing more desperate by the minute, she was still praying for some opportunity to present itself when they turned into the yard of an ancient, low-built tavern faintly proclaiming on a weathered board that it was the Duck and Dandy-boat.

'Come.' Oliver released her arm only to grip her wrist and pull her after him as he descended on to the muddy cobbles.

There was no one about in the yard and the ease with which Oliver propelled her to the open door told her the futility of struggling against him.

The doorway gave entrance to a wide, low-ceilinged passage, its panelled walls black with age and grime. The air here was as thick and stale as though it, too, belonged to the distant past.

A man came through a door at the far end of the passage as they entered. Short and broad, wrapped round in a scarred greasy leather apron, he seemed designed to match the inn. A certain look of hard authority on his cragged face suggested the landlord rather than a hireling. He was perhaps fifty years old, but written into his face there was also the suggestion of a time-out-of-mind acquaintance with all there was to know of humanity's baser instincts. Briefly, incuriously, his gaze ranged over Elaine before it turned to Oliver and he jerked his head

196

upward as if in confirmation of some previously made arrangement.

There was no help to be looked for in that quarter, Elaine saw,
and Oliver's bruising grip on her arm was already forcing her
towards a broad flight of stairs.

At the top of these, a short passage was flanked by two closed
doors and ended in another through which they entered a long,
low-ceilinged room, wainscotted like the entrance passage and lit
by a wide latticed window at the far end. Uncarpeted, the room
contained only a rickety, centrally placed table, a heavy court-
cupboard standing against the right-hand wall and two benches
placed end to end against the opposite wall. There was nothing
in the room to hint at the room's common use.

Once inside, Oliver released Elaine but remained guardian to
the door which he had closed behind them. As much to distance
herself from him, as for any other reason, Elaine walked the
length of the room to the window. Sunlight reflected from a fast-
moving, ebb-tide filled the room with moving light and spangled
the panelling. That the tavern was built on the very edge of the
river was obvious and looking out through the old, uneven glass,
she saw a narrow balcony which appeared to overhang the water.
Casements at either end of the window gave access to the
balcony over low sills. Beyond the balcony's jut she could just see
the end of a skiff which, caught by the river's flow, stretched its
painter to full length as though eager to be off. Upstream to her
right, lay London Bridge, long bereft of its ancient housing. A
trapped bee, buzzing dejectedly against an immovable diamond of
glass, drew her attention. Perhaps it was an unconscious fellow-
feeling that made her unlatch the window and the bee, powered
by relief, winged strongly away.

'You can't fly and I doubt you can swim,' Oliver taunted her,
from his end of the room.

She turned, leaving the window open. He was right. The possibility of escape that way had crossed her mind but it had been no more than a faint hope. 'Why should I need to?' she challenged.

He started towards her, a look of gloating pleasure on his face, but halted as hurried footsteps sounded in the passage beyond the door. He looked back, his expression untroubled, expectant.

Who came in was far beyond any guess Elaine might have made and it was immediately evident that the newcomer was as stunned to see her as she was him.

CHAPTER EIGHTEEN

'*M*iss *Marney*! How are you come—'
Léon Dacier broke off his exclamation to swing his
gaze between Elaine and Oliver and back. Then, with a very
Gallic mock blow to the head, he said in a tone of astonishment,
'*Marney*! You are *allié* . . . related?'

'We're cousins,' Oliver said before Elaine could answer. And
then in frowning suspicion, asked unnecessarily, 'You know each
other?'

'Yes.' Dacier's puzzled gaze remained fixed on Elaine as
though he found it hard to believe her relationship with the other
man.

Pressure of time forced Oliver to dismiss the nudge of disquiet
the information gave him. He had the mastery here and he would
see it recognized. 'Well . . . what news? Did you bring it off this
time?' he demanded impatiently.

Dacier turned from Elaine, his expression darkening. 'No. All
is at an end and we must go *maintenant* – with quickness!'

'*Ha*! So there's a hue and cry after you, is there? Well, my
friend, before we can go there's an obstacle to be removed from
our road. My cousin, there, knows too much.'

Dacier's startled glance swung to Elaine and as quickly back to
Oliver. 'What do you say?'

'I say it's our lives against hers. A brace of pistols, you told me. Unless you fired them both, there she is, a target you can't miss with the river beyond the window for easy disposal.' When Dacier remained motionless, he snorted contempt. 'If you haven't the nerve, lend me a weapon. Either way we don't move from here until she's out of the way. And keep in mind, Frenchman, that I'm your safe-conduct to the coast.'

Dacier frowned and slid his right hand into a pocket. 'The noise?'

'All here are deaf as adders.'

Dacier caught the meaning without understanding the reference. He nodded.

Elaine stood fixed, defenceless and disbelieving. The two men stood between her and the door and she had small chance of reaching the river given the encumbrance of her skirts. She watched the lieutenant draw a pistol from his pocket and look down at it. Long moments passed before he cocked the weapon, the click loud in the silent room.

Oliver growled roughly, 'Get on with it if you hope to see France again! A prince or a woman – what difference?'

Dacier looked up. Smiled thinly. '*Vous vous trompez.*'

He brought the gun up levelling it at Elaine with the unhurried confidence of a practised marksman. But swiftly, smoothly, his movement curved past her to reach Oliver and was infinitesimally adjusted in the moment before he fired. Astonished, Oliver lurched back two untidy steps and fell.

Too certain of his marksmanship over so small a distance, Dacier regarded Oliver's unmoving form for no more than a moment before he turned to Elaine. 'You will not grieve for such a one, I think,' he said calmly.

Elaine's shocked mind, held only one thought: *He told Oliver he was mistaken, but Oliver did not understand.*

Each engrossed in their own way, neither Dacier nor Elaine had registered the sounds of another arrival. Dacier was walking towards Elaine, had almost reached her when the door was thrust open to thud back against wall.

Dacier spun round. Softly, on a note of almost amused resignation, he breathed, '*You. . . .*'

'*Lui-même.*' Cato's gaze gathered detail in one swift sweep of the room. It came to rest on Elaine for several seconds, cold, blank, unwavering, then returned to the lieutenant as though he had no difficulty in wiping her presence from his mind.

Dacier half raised the gun he held. Cato merely shook his head. '*C'est fini, mon ami.* Your gun is empty, mine is not and there are two troopers in the passage, four more below stairs.' He brought his right hand into view showing the pistol he held. Gesturing with it towards Oliver's body, he asked simply, 'Why? He was your conductor.'

Dacier shrugged, his expression showing the depth of his contempt. '*Vile canaille!*' he said, as if that were sufficient explanation.

'And His Royal Highness? Why such a thirst for *his* blood?'

'Your country *humilier* . . . makes humble our Emperor. I do what I can to *redresser* – to make even. But for you, *m'sieur*—' He shook his head.

'Well, you tried.'

'Once, *you* I could have killed. *Sans doute.* Why did I not!'

'An error of judgement.'

'*Absolument!*' Dacier shrugged and dropped his useless pistol back into a pocket. 'And *la conséquence?*'

'What do you expect, Lieutenant? An attempt on the Regent's life cannot be less than a hanging matter.'

Elaine uttered a small, shocked gasp of protest, saw Dacier's body stiffen in repudiation.

'*Hanging!*' he said with abhorrence.

'We have no guillotine in this country,' Cato told him brusquely.

201

Drawing himself erect, suddenly very French and with just a touch of bravado, Dacier said, '*Vive l'Empereur!*' Less theatrically, he added wryly, 'Almost, I succeed. Perhaps to do your country a service in removing your so *impopulaire* regent.'

'That is a privilege we prefer to keep for ourselves. And we have abandoned murder as a means.' Cato's easy tone covered an unyielding authority. His search had come to a proper end. He was as certain of what would follow as a tiger that has stalked its prey into a cleft among rocks.

Elaine, however, foresaw violence, for she did not believe that in the end, Dacier would submit tamely even under the threat of Cato's gun. And as Oliver had suggested, he might have a second – and loaded – pistol. Either man could die or be badly wounded and every feeling rebelled against the thought. Dacier was the friend with whom she had laughed, danced, even flirted a little, but more importantly, he was the man to whom she owed her life twice over. Worse even than the fear of his being shot was to think of him choking out his own life in a brutal and degrading end.

And Cato. . . . But where he was concerned thought and feeling were too confused to attempt examination. What stood clear was that she saw a chance for Dacier to escape. With her help. But success would mean Cato being robbed of his prisoner. How could she do that to him?

How could she not? She closed the small distance between herself and Dacier.

Quiet as her movement had been, it drew Cato's attention. He looked at her now, his granite-grey eyes as hard as the crystalline stone. His voice rough with a contempt he had not shown towards the Frenchman, he said, 'You stand now where you should, madam. Where you are likely to stand when you share your companion's end.'

'No!' Dacier protested with fierce, astonished indignation. 'You mistake! Mam'selle Marney came – was brought – by that *monstre*, her cousin. For *me* to shoot!'

Cato heard that as no more than a gallant attempt to shelter the woman. Returning his attention to Dacier, he said, 'Was she to go with you to France? You'll find the lady free with her favours.' And the rankling corollary to that was that if she was giving up Braxted for Dacier, he himself was left a very poor third in the tally.

Elaine forestalled Dacier's scornful response. 'Do not trouble yourself to reply. Mr Raffen would still believe what he chooses.'

But the moment for treacherous action had come. Her heart thudding, she laid a hand on Dacier's sleeve, bent her head towards him and whispered, 'The window behind us. A boat below the balcony. Go!'

He stared at her, his brown eyes lighting to fierce hope but narrowing as swiftly to a frown. 'You?' he breathed.

Her fingers tightened compellingly on his arm. 'I am safe. Believe me. *Go quickly!*'

The chance to escape was irresistible. He compressed all he could of gratitude into his last look at her, swung round and leapt for the open window.

Cato had watched with grudging eyes what he saw as a moment of intimacy between hard-pressed lovers. He had not heard what was said and his suspicion was entirely misdirected. Dacier's sudden movement caught him unawares though he recovered quickly. Raising his pistol, he started forward, but there was more than half the room to cross and Elaine moving towards him was blocking his view of the lieutenant. Intent on the man, he did not guess Elaine's purpose until she thrust the rickety table across his path. Tilting, it struck him across the thighs to send him stumbling back and his finger tightening on the trigger, the gun discharged into the ceiling. But he had not fallen, and in one more desperate bid to slow his passage, Elaine thrust herself in his path.

Cato flung her roughly aside, all his attention on Dacier. But she had given the lieutenant time to clear window, balcony and rail. As Cato crossed the sill, the lieutenant dropped gently into the skiff and freed it from its mooring. Seized by the current~ the boat was skimming away before Dacier could even pick up the oars.

His empty pistol now useless, Cato crossed back into the room. The sweep of his arm had sent Elaine staggering off balance to fall to her knees. Balked, coldly furious, he watched her rise to her feet without offering help.

The bleakness of his expression told Elaine there could be no forgiveness for what she had done . . . that he could not have borne at that moment even to touch her. If she had ever had the smallest faith in the assurance of her immunity given to Dacier, she lost it now.

The sound of the shot had brought the sergeant and a trooper in from the passage in a rush. Cato turned from her to give rapid instructions for the pursuit of Dacier and the disposal of Oliver's body.

When the men had clattered out again a silence as intense as a killing frost fell on the room.

Savouring to the dregs the bitter cup she had chosen to drink, Elaine realized that with Oliver dead and Dacier out of reach, there was no one to testify to her entire innocence until the last few minutes. What she had done then might be enough to bring down on her the penalty with which Cato Raffen had threatened her. She did not know and for the racked and tormented present, she did not care.

The look Cato turned on her now was an insult though he spoke with icy dispassion. 'You connive at the escape of a man who has murdered your kinsman, who is an enemy of your country and who would have murdered the Regent if he could. Is there anything from which you shrink, Miss Marney?'

She would not let him know the cost of her action to herself, but gathered all of what strength she had left to keep her voice steady and say with withering sweetness, 'I leave it to you to judge.'

Still in a flatly expressionless voice, he returned, 'You will be fortunate indeed, if others judge you differently.'

As though compelled, as though to save her life she could not at this moment hold her tongue, she said, 'Lieutenant Dacier was a Frenchman with a Frenchman's view of the matter. As for Oliver—' She shuddered and let that go. 'Perhaps villainy is largely a point of view.'

Treating the words as meaningless, he merely gestured towards the door. 'Come. I'll take you back to Sheffney House.'

Goaded beyond bearing, she asked in the sweet injurious tone she had used before, 'Not to Newgate? Or perhaps the Tower?'

'You would be wise not to try my patience too far, Miss Marney. I can as easily lodge you in a bridewell among the drabs of the streets. You may find yourself there yet. You are in very real danger of ending with a rope around that white neck of yours. Believe me!'

He was unmoved, unmovable, and the most necessary thing in life for her had become her need to strike fire from him. 'How can I not believe you?' she asked. ' After all, you are the chief witness for the prosecution.'

Something flickered behind his eyes. 'Are you trying to put your neck in a noose?'

Far beyond the reach of caution now, she laughed, though it was a small, breathless travesty of laughter. 'What need? I leave it to you to do.'

She had what she wanted. His face changed. He stepped towards her and all strength drained from her.

Having sown the wind, in the face of the whirlwind, for the first time in her life, she fainted.

CHAPTER NINETEEN

For whatever sins she had committed, to sit beside Cato Raffen in silence throughout the drive back to Sheffney House, must surely be punishment enough, Elaine thought despairingly.

She had recovered from her faint to find herself still lying on the floor, the dry, alien taste of brandy in her mouth. Cato Raffen knelt beside her, one arm supporting her head and shoulders, a glass in his other hand. As she looked up he had turned to hand the glass to a tall trooper who stood nearby gazing down at her with open curiosity. That avid look spurred on her return to full consciousness and she had made an effort to sit up. At once Cato, rising to his feet, had drawn her up with him and in one smooth, continuous action lifted her into his arms, carried her down the stairs and out to the chaise in which she had arrived at the tavern with Oliver. It was all done with cold despatch, as though he had never held her in his arms in a quite different way, never kissed her, never looked at her with loving warmth, or even with the consuming fury that was the last thing she had seen before she fainted.

Her senses were still tending to swim unpleasantly and she felt sick. She was aware of Cato glancing at her from time to time, but it was in a detached way devoid of sympathy.

When they reached Sheffney House, she accepted the hand he offered to help her down from the carriage because without it she might have fallen. She would take no further aid from him, though it took iron determination to walk up the house steps and keep her legs from failing her.

Alerted by the sound of the knocker, Gertie was in the hall to meet them when Newbald opened the door to them.

'Elaine! Oh, my dear, where have you been! We have all been in such alarm.' Her anxious gaze flowed over Elaine, from her pale, exhausted face, down over her lilac-coloured grenadine gown, soiled beyond recovery from its double contact with the tavern's unswept floor. 'Has there been an accident?'

Elaine, at the end of her endurance, groped through her numbed mind and said, 'Mr Raffen will tell you. Forgive me, Gertie, but I must go—' She gestured towards the stairs, remembered her dubious position and turned shadowed eyes to Cato. With a last flicker of spirit, she said, 'With your permission, of course, sir.'

His mouth thinned to a narrow line. Matching her intransigence he inclined his head in stiff, provocative assent. He watched her walk away across the hall, saw her stumble on the first stair and fought the impulse to go after her, take her in his arms again and carry her up the stairs to her bed. Cold reason told him it was misdirected compassion: she deserved to suffer the consequence of what she did. Unreason added she was the more deserving because he had loved her.

Gertie was close to being open-mouthed. Her astonished gaze swinging between the two took in Newbald standing monumentally in the background and prompted her to say, 'Send Polly Cutts to take some wine up to Miss Marney and attend to her needs.' Then to Cato, her hazel eyes bright and sharp with questions, she said, 'Come with me.'

The moment the door of the Primrose Parlour closed on them

she swung round on him. '*Why* in heaven's name should Elaine ask *your* permission to go to her room, Cato?'

He let several moments pass before he answered her and in that time she thought she had never seen so bleak, so implacable a look on his face.

At last he said, 'As I expected, there was an attempt on the Regent's life this morning.'

'The Regent!' Gertie frowned her impatience at this seeming irrelevance. 'What can his affairs have to say to Elaine!'

'More than you expect. The would-be assassin proved to be Lieutenant Léon Dacier. He came close to a success I was only just in time to prevent. I had him in my hand, too, but he broke free when the ever-inquisitive crowd breached the barriers to get close to what was happening. But I knew his route to safety, the first stage of which was a low, riverside tavern. I was close on his heels and there I found him in company with Miss Marney and her cousin, Oliver Marney. Oliver, however, was dead.'

'This is beyond me!' Gertie gasped. Looking stunned, she plumped down into a chair.

'Marney was shot by Dacier as I was arriving. Miss Marney appeared to have little interest in the event. Indeed, her only interest appeared to be in the lieutenant.'

Gertie closed her eyes; opened them to say, 'For pity's sake sit down, Cato. I haven't begun to understand.'

When he was seated, she said, 'Why should Lieutenant Dacier want to kill the Regent, connected to the Stapfords as he is? And what could Elaine have to do with any of it? As for Oliver Marney Elaine never could like him. She tolerated him because I persuaded her that as her only kinsman she should. Though lately, I had begun to think I had made a sad mistake.'

'Dacier concealed the fact that he is an ardent Bonapartist. His intention was to avenge his Emperor's downfall.'

Gertie shook her head in wonder. 'He was such a charming

209

young man, one met him everywhere. How could it be!'

'For all his English connections, he was a Frenchman. And a French soldier. His hero is Napoleon, as ours is Wellington.'

'But what had Oliver Marney to do with it? I cannot believe he cared a jot for Bonaparte's fortunes!'

'Only in as much as they brought him profit. Under cover of the carrier business he owns, Marney ran a well-rewarded trade conveying escaping prisoners of war to his smuggling friends who took them on across the Channel. He was what was known as a 'conductor', the man responsible for making all the overland travelling arrangements for vehicles, clothing, overnight stops, general safety, until Lydd or Rye was reached, or any other port that may have been chosen. Dacier was no longer a prisoner of war, but a special case involving high risks. Marney must have had some knowledge of what Dacier intended. A very large sum would have been demanded to convey him to safety. It was a groom in the employ of a certain lady living in Tunbridge Wells who gave the original warning of an attempt on the Regent's life. He chanced to feel a certain indignation – *not* that the Regent was to be murdered – but that a *Frenchman* should have the insolence to undertake it. His brother is – was . . .' He skimmed past the change of tense, remembering the manner in which the brother had brought about his own death outside the gates of Ringlestone – 'was in the smuggling trade in Rye and let slip some information when the two were drinking together. The groom took some risk in passing on even the little he knew because the smugglers inflict barbarous punishments on those who betray them.'

'But *Elaine! Elaine!* How can she have been involved!'

Cato was silent, looking inward, his expression closed, grim. At last he said, 'If her presence at the tavern with the two men did not condemn her, the fact that it was by her contrivance Dacier escaped me the second time does.' With dark and bitter emphasis, he repeated, 'Her determined contrivance.' He related Elaine's part in the escape.

Gertie regarded him with troubled eyes. It seemed to her that the help Elaine had given Dacier mattered more to him than the man's escape, deeply though that must gall him. She said quietly, 'Her reason would be that Dacier saved her life. At very least, saved her from dreadful injury. As you know.'

He tossed her an impatient look. 'Her reasons alter nothing. Remember the life put in jeopardy was the Regent's.'

'But you say Léon Dacier shot Oliver Marney who was to help him to reach the coast. . . . Why should he do that? It is all so confusing! How did Elaine come to be with Oliver? She said no word of seeing him today. He did not call here and Elaine was not dressed for going out. The maid who waits on her knows nothing. It was what worried us so when she could not be found in the house. It was all so mysterious. The only thing—' She broke off.

'The only thing?'

'Yesterday she borrowed a hundred pounds from me. All I had in the house. She was not very clear why she wanted so much when quarter day is almost upon us. But Cato, you must have asked her to explain why she was where she was. What did she tell you.'

He was poised to answer her when he found that he could not recall a single question he had asked Miss Marney. It had not been questions he had thrown at her, but taunts and accusations. With devilish timing, Dacier's words returned to him, '*Mam'selle Marney came – was brought – by that* monstre. . . .' And then, confounding him further, some inner ear resonated with what else the lieutenant had said, '*For me to shoot!*' Words that had made no impact at the time and which he had dismissed with the rest. They made no more sense now, but the first worm of doubt coiled its way unpleasantly into his mind.

Watching him keen-eyed, Gertie said, 'I have the strangest feeling that you *want* to believe Elaine guilty of something. Indeed, almost anything. It is a large change in a man who told me she meant more to him than he cared to acknowledge.'

'I have since told you I found she was not what I thought her.'

'And you want to punish her for it?'

He stared at her in angry silence, then said explosively, 'No!' and knew that he lied. To cover it, he said, 'What I want is beside the point. What is certain is that she helped Dacier to escape and is accountable for it.'

'I understand the importance of Dacier's escape to you. But do you really want to see him hang? In the end, he did the Regent no harm.'

'Women's logic, Gertie. His intention was to kill. He made two attempts. Perhaps more.'

'To avenge Napoleon, you said. That may make him a villain in England, but there are many in France who would think him a hero. I ask you again, Cato, are you anxious to see him hang?'

'Oh, damn you, Gertie! And that's without apology.' He was on his feet again, restive and irritated. He swung away from her. Swung back. 'I hardly knew the man. Met him fewer than half a dozen times. No, I have no personal wish to see Dacier hang, but what does that count for? We're talking about the attempted murder of the man who, but for being crowned, is this country's king.'

'No, Cato. Or not that alone. We're talking about Elaine Marney and what you intend towards her. I don't know what lies between you besides what happened today, but I think you should take careful thought before you let the matter pass beyond your management. Can you really want to harm her?'

Again he stared at her, the lines of his face drawn taut. With a kind of hard-held violence, he said, 'It will not rest with me. My part is only to inform Braxted of the day's happenings. So you

212

have no real cause for concern. Beyond all doubt, Miss Marney will be safe in his hands.'

Gertie's eyes opened wide at the biting certainty of his tone. 'How can you be so sure?'

'Suffice it to say that I am. And for the present that is *all* I mean to say—'

On that sour note, he left.

Gertie tussled with the tangle a while before taking herself upstairs to hear Elaine's version of the day's events. But by that time Elaine was deep in the sleep of exhaustion.

It was two hours later when Elaine woke from the black oblivion into which she had fallen and, throwing off the quilt with which Polly Cutts had covered her after removing her soiled gown, rose from the bed. Washed and in a clean gown, she found herself physically stronger but her mind dulled by a weight of apathy. As she walked down the stairs her lack of feeling was such that if she had found a soldier escort waiting below to take her to some grim grey prison she would not have cared. There was, however, only Gertie waiting for her, concerned, impatient, and deeply curious.

Elaine's flat recountal of what had happened had the ring of truth, melodramatic and extraordinary though it was. It was bizarre enough, but it fitted both the circumstances and the girl far more naturally than Cato's dark reading of events.

Speaking of Dacier, Elaine said, 'I know his intention was bad and I don't know how I would have acted had he succeeded in killing the Regent. But the Regent was unharmed and when the lieutenant shot Oliver it was done for my sake and at cost to himself because Oliver was his safe conduct to the coast. I could not bear to think of his being hanged. I *had* to give him a chance to escape! As for Oliver himself – I find I can feel nothing. Nothing at all.' She was silent a moment then said with a savage little laugh, 'Mr Raffen has a very different view of what

213

happened, as I am sure he has told you. He hopes to see me hanged, with or without Lieutenant Dacier.'

'My dear!' Gertie was shocked. 'Do not speak so! It is altogether too wild an exaggeration.'

Elaine shook her head. 'No, Gertie, it is not. It is what he promised me. And he sounded very much as though he wished it.'

What she had been told of the day's events had seemed to Gertie so highly coloured as to be unreal and it was only now that the possibility of Elaine standing in real danger came home to her. But danger through Cato? She could not believe it. But once it was out of his hands, what then? She remembered his bitter words asserting Braxted's readiness to protect the girl. What did he know about James and Elaine that she did not? Was jealousy the reason Cato was so embittered?

She said distressfully, 'My dear, I don't wish to pry, but it would help me to understand why Cato is so out of reason angry with you if you would tell me what has come between you.'

Not knowing what that was, was the cruellest part of all that was changed between them and tears sprang to Elaine's eyes. Furiously, she blinked them back. 'If I knew, I would tell you, Gertie. But I don't. I had come to think he held me in some affection. Then suddenly everything changed. He went to the far extreme and I don't know why.'

She really did not know, Gertie saw. She said wonderingly, 'He told *me* that he loved you. That he hoped to marry you. But he has not said what caused him to change his mind. But what of you, Elaine? What are your feelings?'

Elaine's looked at her, her chin defiantly lifted, her tear-glazed eyes brilliant. 'Don't be concerned for me, Gertie. Fortunately, Mr Raffen put a speedy end to my regard for him.'

And that I suspect, thought Gertie with an inward sigh, is the only lie she has told me this morning.

214

A few rumours of a small commotion at the Prince's last review of the year floated about town. Some favoured the idea that an attack on His Royal Highness had been intended; others that it had been a grossly misplaced culmination to a private quarrel between two gentlemen, one of whom had rushed upon and scuffled with the other. The worst feature of the matter had been the crowd breaking through the barriers and alarming a number of ladies, one or two of whom had succumbed to hysterics. No real harm had been done however, and public interest in the matter soon died.

No news reached Sheffney House in the next three days of anything to do with Léon Dacier. Nor were there any immediate consequences for Elaine relating to the events into which Oliver had dragged her. But living daily in expectation of some dire result tore at her nerves. Her chief concern was how any ensuing scandal might reflect on Gertie who had presented her to society as her friend and protégée. Gertie shrugged that off with contempt, firmly repudiating any idea of Elaine leaving Sheffney House. She could not, *would not*, she declared, believe that Cato's actions would match his threatening words. But her nerves, too, felt the strain and in a weak moment she wondered whether even Cato might not yield to the temptations that beset an angry, jealous man.

And where was James Valdoe in all this? What part, Gertie would very much like to be told, was that astute patrician playing?

The fourth morning after Elaine's return from the Duck and Dandy-boat provided them both with welcome relief. Hearing an unusual commotion in the hall, Gertie and Elaine came into it together to see, standing amid a litter of boxes, a tall, confident-looking man, whose upright, slightly burly figure put even

Newbald's imposing presence in the shade. A bustle of footmen was treading up and down the steps from the road into the house unloading larger trunks from the heavy berlin standing outside.

Approaching this august person, Gertie said coolly, 'So here you are! A tardy return and then come without the least warning! You can have little expectation of a warm welcome, my lord.'

By which prickly greeting Elaine recognized that here at last was the long awaited, eagerly looked for Earl of Sheffney.

His Lordship, dealt summarily with his crabbed reception. Trampling over society's belief that a decent nonchalance should always be maintained between married couples, he strode to meet his wife and sweep her into a bearlike hug. Heedless of Elaine, butler, footmen and any other possible onlookers, he proceeded to kiss her heartily and at length.

Which his lady in no way discouraged.

CHAPTER TWENTY

The Marquis of Braxted, calling at Sheffney House two days after the earl's return, informed Newbald he wished to have a private word with His Lordship and was shown into the library where Sheffney soon joined him.

'Good to see you back. I was beginning to think you unable to tear yourself away from Paris or Vienna, or wherever it was you were last disporting yourself.'

Sheffney snorted disgust. 'Either place it's the same. You'd think that dancing all night and sleeping all day was the entire purpose for which the nations' leaders are gathered together. To accomplish anything at all has been a damnably slow and tedious business.'

'Yet, from what I have heard, you are to be congratulated on having carried through your own mission to the admiration of all.'

'At the cost of being absent from my own affairs three times longer than necessary. I can tell you I'm damned glad to be back!' Sheffney studied his visitor with shrewd, heavy-lidded blue eyes for a moment. 'I have been expecting you, James, and not just to welcome me back and butter my toast for me. Take a seat and I'll pour us both a glass of Madeira before you tell me why else you are here.'

Braxted's level brows quirked upward. 'Developed a gift for clairvoyance, Charles? Or are you speaking from information given?'

Charles, about to hand him a filled glass, paused momentarily, held by something in the other man's tone, but then, completing his action, said only, 'Let us see if we have the same thing in mind.'

Braxted gazed down into his wine as though seeking a beginning. When he looked up again, he said, 'You will have made the acquaintance of your wife's young friend and protégée, Elaine Marney. . . .'

Sheffney nodded. 'Yes. It is about her I was expecting – or perhaps hoping – you would speak. Go on.'

'She is my daughter. My natural daughter.'

Sheffney looked stunned. 'Good God! That is *not* what I expected you to say! Gertie has been in a worry—' He broke off and lowered himself into a chair facing Braxted. 'Well, let that rest. I imagine you have more to tell me.'

'An old story, as you may guess, and far from uncommon. At the time it began you were thinking of marriage and spending much of your time in Dorset, so knew nothing of it. But I, too, had fallen in love. . . .' He went on to tell Sheffney what he had told Elaine at the Lawrenses' ball.

Watching his friend's face, Sheffney saw that for all Braxted's even recital strong feelings lay not far beneath the surface. Quietly he lifted himself out of his chair and refilled the other man's glass.

'What led you to these discoveries?' Sheffney asked after a lengthy pause. 'What Gertie has said to me does not make it appear you could have known when you first met Elaine Marney.'

'No. Though it was her remarkable likeness to her mother that first fixed my attention on her. In looks, she is Marianne's counterpart and her name confirmed relationship. But it was the

218

dissimilarities in character that held my interest. Marianne had a dovelike gentleness. Not so Elaine. Her mind is stronger. She makes her own judgements. The first questions opened in my mind when I read the initials on her dropped handkerchief and learned that her second name was one of mine. It prompted a question which, answered, told me she was a little older than I had believed.'

He told Sheffney the rest of the story, of his journey to Dorset, his tracking to its source the money paid to Joseph Marney and other details, reluctantly revealed but highly relevant, prised from the son of his father's former man of business.

'It was knowing what I was looking for that made it possible despite the passage of years,' he ended.

'And now it is beyond doubt?'

'Beyond doubt. Elaine is nearly a year older than I thought her and Marianne was indisputably a virgin until I seduced her. I have sifted the matter to the last possible grain.'

'So what do you propose for your daughter now?'

'Whatever is in her best interest. If I acknowledge her, it proclaims her illegitimacy. Because I am not married, adoption would be no advantage to her given society's delight in creating scandal. My interest in her has been public and, I do not doubt, misinterpreted. Whatever happens, I will see she is made secure from now on. I'm proud of her, Charles.'

'Gertie knows nothing of this and for that reason has had grave doubts in your regard.'

'When I first told Elaine, I asked her not to speak of it to anyone until I had thought how best to guard her interests. I am telling you now, Charles, because I have a favour to ask that needs your sanction before Gertie's.'

'Your daughter needs a home, a background, until you have made other arrangements?' Sheffney guessed shrewdly.

'Yes.'

'I see no reason why Miss— Miss Elaine should suffer for your sins,' Sheffney said dryly. 'She is welcome to remain with us as long as she will. At the moment she does not plan to do so. We move down to Bredescourt at the end of next week and she has said she will not go with us.'

Braxted's dark eyes gleamed with amusement. 'Tell her, if you will, that it is her father's wish and command that she accompany you into the country.'

'Will she heed you?'

'I hope the novelty of having a kinder father to command her than the one she thought was hers may charm her as much as it charms me to have a daughter to command.' He glanced at a nearby clock and stood up. 'I must go. In an hour or so, I must set out for Brighton. Six days ago, at a late review in Hyde Park, there was an attempt on Prinny's life. An attempt foiled by Gertie's friend, Cato Raffen. Did you know?'

'Yes. Castlereagh had the news passed to me. A Frenchman who, possibly, has made good his escape to his own country.'

Braxted nodded. 'Which Raffen sees as less than perfect fulfilment of what he undertook. It appears to vex him sorely.' He looked as though he meant to add to that, changed his mind and said instead, 'I am required to assure Prinny of the unlikeliness of another such attempt. He, being no fool, will know my words to be hollow, but for want of better, will accept them. *Noblesse oblige!*'

They shook hands and were walking to the door when Braxted stopped to say, 'You said you were expecting me to speak of Elaine, but not in the particular connection I did.'

It was a question and Sheffney considered his answer before speaking. If Braxted knew that Elaine Marney was involved in Dacier's escape, would he not have said? Perhaps not. But some telltale hint of concern for his daughter might have been expected to escape him; a hint that a longtime friend would not miss.

Smoothly diplomatic, Sheffney returned, 'It is no longer to the point. What you have said and not said, has adequately covered the matter.'

'Well, it is all a long way from my fears and supposing,' said Gertie astonished by what her husband had told her. 'And you say it is quite beyond doubt?'

'So he assures me.'

'So many changes of fortune, Elaine must wonder who, or what she is!' While shaking her head over that she found another puzzle. 'When he was talking of her part in that business with Dacier, Cato said she would be safe in James's hands. But how did he know? And why should it make him so angry?'

'You may be surprised to learn that Raffen does not appear to have said anything to James about Miss Marney's presence at the tavern.'

'If he has not, it is a miracle in itself. He was so bitter. So seemingly bent on her being called to account.'

'Well, it's their problem. Leave them to it. The girl's life is going to change radically one way or another. If Raffen has made her unhappy, I've no doubt she will find compensation enough before long. Braxted will see to it that she marries well. As for Raffen, he'll have to swallow his bile. Where is he now, by the way?'

Gertie sighed. 'Yesterday, I had the briefest of notes to say he was leaving town to go down to Eldenshaw. His brother Julian is, at last, about to depart this world. Cato will be Lord Meldreth when he returns. But with all the problems Julian has ensured he inherits, I imagine that will not be soon.'

Hidden in the green and gracious Surrey countryside near Dorking, Bredescourt had seen many changes since its small beginning as a cruck hall in the late fourteenth century. By some

221

alchemy of time and grace, it and its numerous and sometimes whimsical additions had united into a serenely happy whole and the house sat now at the end of a long drive winding through magnificently wooded parkland with what might be thought an air of certainty of pleasing the eye.

So Elaine thought seeing it for the first time in the amber glow of a sunny late September afternoon. A moment later, the full view was lost as the Sheffney travelling carriage swung into the last curve of the drive and then under a pedimented archway into a low-walled forecourt. The horses were drawn to a halt before the wide, iron-studded door set back in a stone porch of obvious antiquity. Instantly the door opened and two footmen emerged to let down the steps of the carriage and assist its occupants to alight.

Standing on the flags before following Gertie into the house, Elaine thought that if she had any dreams left to weave, Bredescourt, unblushingly romantic in appearance, would be just the place to weave them. But that kind of foolishness was at an end and she had no intention of indulging herself in such a way again.

With an amusement very like her father's, she had complied with his wish for her to remain with Gertie and her husband, endorsed as it had been by their assurances of her being truly welcome. Though she had resolutely put the recent past behind her, she was glad to escape from London and to have a physical distance set between her and reminders of all that had happened to her there. She needed a period of tranquillity, a respite from change, time to recover some of her old certainties.

She soon found that, in the country, the Sheffneys kept to a style of living that had an Arcadian simplicity compared with what prevailed in Berkeley Square. She slipped into it easily and found it suited her. But restful as it was, and for all her resolution to put the past – which meant Cato Raffen – behind her, forgetfulness and the ease of heart and mind she hoped for did not come quickly. What she could be grateful for was that life ran smoothly with little happening that was not expected.

Towards the end of October, she received a letter from Léon Dacier, sent on from Sheffney House. Now safely in France, he offered his fervent thanks for her help in his escape. He had been relieved to learn, he wrote without disclosing his source, that she had suffered no obvious reprisal and hoped she had borne none.

About the same time, Gertie received a letter from Cato confirming his brother's death. Written with less than his usual brotherly freedom, he also confirmed what she had anticipated, that restoring Eldenshaw was his immediate concern and overseeing it would keep him in Rosemorton for some time to come. Except that first he must make a necessary visit to London and expected to be there for a week soon after this letter reached her. He made no proposal for coming into Surrey, gave little other news and ended with his compliments to Lord Barlborough. The omissions spoke more loudly than the cool tone of the letter.

The Marquis of Braxted had always been a frequent visitor to Bredescourt. Now that it housed his daughter, his visits became even more frequent.

His visits were a pleasure to Elaine and for each of them they were voyages of discovery. From liking on both sides affection grew easily and exchanged memories built something of a linked past.

For a time Elaine waited for her father to raise the subject of her part in what had happened at the Duck and Dandy-boat. But his silence on the subject continued and a day or two after Dacier's letter arrived, she decided to open the matter herself. Of the letter itself she said nothing, but on that cool and windy day when they were walking together in the grounds of Bredescourt through an avenue of tall clipped yews, she mentioned the tavern by name. Braxted turned to her in astonishment.

'What do you know of that place?'

'I know what happened there. I was there myself. Took part. Were you not told?'

'No.'

They stopped walking and stared at one another, busy with their thoughts.

So, for all his threats, Cato had not even hinted at her presence at the inn. What *had* he told the Marquis? Elaine wondered. It seemed clear enough that whatever he had said about Oliver, he had entirely omitted any reference to herself from his report. *But why? Gertie!* Yes, of course, Gertie! she answered her own question. How could she have failed to realize earlier that Cato's long affection for Gertie would put a brake on what he told the marquis! Once his fury over Dacier's escape had cooled, he would have become aware that any scandal resulting from his revelations would draw in the Countess of Sheffney, if only for having a protégée and house-guest involved in an attempt to murder the Regent.

Her confidence in her new-found father was strong enough to allow her to tell him the story of her part in the events: her part, but without the wicked exchanges between herself and Cato Raffen.

Braxted thought it over in silence for what seemed a long time before asking, 'You engineered the escape of an enemy of the state?'

'Yes, I suppose I did.'

'It was not a dilemma to you?'

'No.' She told him her reasons.

'Were you in love with him?'

'No. But I liked him.'

'Was he in love with you?'

She almost said *no* before she remembered her brief tête-à-tête

224

with Dacier at the Bouveries' musical evening and said instead, 'Perhaps a little. A very little.'

'It is fortunate the matter was being investigated unofficially. Officialdom would have searched out details more perseveringly. Might not have been willing to leave you out of the reckoning. Could have discounted your motives, in which case the results for you could have been serious, indeed.'

He looked away from her down the remaining length of the yew walk. 'What interests me particularly is why Raffen, or Lord Meldreth as he now is, concealed so much from me. It could not have been to spare my feelings because he can have had no knowledge of our relationship. I remember thinking when he made his report to me that he was more troubled by the way the affair ended than seemed quite natural. Perhaps it was because you, a woman, had been the means—' He broke off, said musingly, 'Was there not some attraction between you at one time? Did robbing him of his triumph in capturing Dacier end it?'

She shook her head. 'No. *That* ended some days before. My helping Dacier escape simply confirmed and hardened a changed opinion of me. I cannot pretend to understand what caused the change. It happened suddenly and completely and was so extreme that when he found me at the tavern with Lieutenant Dacier and Oliver he was deaf to all explanation of how I came to be there. His silence over my presence at the Duck and Dandy-boat can only have been for the sake of Gertie and her husband.'

'Not all the reason, I think. He would know I should protect them to my limit. If it is any comfort to you, consider it possible he had some thought for you, too.'

Elaine held too great a tally against Cato Raffen to consider any such thing. She did not dispute it, however, merely answering him with a small, wintry smile and a shake of her head and the subject was dropped.

225

CHAPTER TWENTY-ONE

*I*n the second week of November, Fanny gave birth to twin girls. Though the babies were healthy and thriving, the double birth had been less easy than Fanny's earlier labours and her recovery was slow.

When, a few days after the event, Elaine and Gertie drove to Highgate to view the babies, a wan Fanny, sunk among pillows, admitted to feeling decidedly *mumpish* and before they departed begged Gertie to lend Elaine to her for a time if Elaine were willing to come.

Elaine consulted Braxted without any real expectation of the visit being denied, and within another week was back with the Woolfords at Bellehaugh.

Since Braxted, still taking pleasure in his unexpected fatherhood, wished to continue to visit her, John and Fanny had now to be told the truth of her parentage. This and the fact that Braxted had settled a larger sum on her than Sarah Marney's fortune amounted to, enabled Elaine to consult John at an early date regarding the disposal of that particular *damnosa hereditas*. She considered she had no real claim to the money for, though she bore the name Marney, she now knew she was unrelated to the family. For that alone, she was grateful. Oliver's readiness to do murder to gain possession of Sarah Marney's

227

money had set the final seal on her dislike of it and of him. Even now, the manner of his death left her numb except for a little late pity for a man whose driving greed had brought him to an early death.

'Because you were born after your mother married Joseph Marney, in the eyes of the law you are Joseph Marney's daughter,' John Woolford had told her. 'In default of any other claimant, you inherit from Oliver and have a right to the money.'

'But I don't want it. And now don't need it.'

'If you insist on giving it away there are a number of worthy charities that would be more than grateful to receive all or part of such a sum.'

'May I leave it in your hands to distribute then?'

To which John Woolford had agreed.

The babies continued to thrive, Fanny began to recover her health and liveliness and to make plans for Christmas in the hope that her sons would not be prevented from returning to enjoy them this year.

By the time Christmas was almost upon them, Elaine felt that she had reached a level plain of feeling. Three months had gone by since the momentous events that had begun on the night of the Lawrenses' ball and which had culminated six days later at the Thames-side tavern. The worst of the cruel surges of emotion had passed and the wicked memories were beginning to submit to her determined refusal to give them more than a moment's anchorage.

Braxted was making plans that forced her to look towards the future. He wanted her to see the home that might have been hers and his pride and interest in her, the growing affection between them, gave her a new confidence. Between the marquis and the Woolfords she was given even less time for brooding than she had had at Bredescourt. She began to put faith in the belief that she would one day be free of all thought of Cato Raffen: Lord

Meldreth was a different person, someone she did not know. A name that did not jolt her when she heard it.

A little before Christmas, a year almost to the day since he had walked into The Griffin at the beginning of that memorable period of ferocious winter weather, Lord Meldreth came to consult John Woolford on a small legal quibble raised by the man who had bought Ringlestones. He had suggested coming to see the lawyer at Bellehaugh as perhaps being more convenient for them both.

His true reason for coming had nothing to do with convenience or legality and everything to do with Elaine Marney. From the time he had pushed open a door to see Elaine in Braxted's arms and hear His Lordship's words, she had lived in his mind, despised, condemned, but enduringly desirable, needed. For that he despised himself.

Gertie had been right when she said he wanted to punish her. But not for Dacier's escape – always and entirely for being of less worth than he had thought. At the wretched tavern where he had found her with Dacier, she had thrown back his anger and contempt with defiance; had by some extraordinary inversion shown *him* contempt. Which was what had driven him to attempt to terrify her. In the end, having succeeded too well, he himself had been punished by the memory of the look on her face in the moment before she fainted. Against that he could set the fact that Braxted had almost lived at Bredescourt since Elaine had gone there with Gertie and her husband. That Gertie should countenance Braxted enjoying his paramour's favours under her roof had shocked him. To learn that the liaison was apparently as easily accepted at Bellehaugh provoked him to a degree of cynicism he knew to be unreasonable given the licentiousness of the age. He had only to consider the Countess of Oxford's well-stocked nursery of mixed fathering, generally known as the

Harleian miscellany, but still tolerated by her husband, Lord Harley. . . .

For all that he held against Elaine Marney, he was here at Bellehaugh, conscious of folly and at the same time unable to escape a little consciousness of some generosity of purpose.

The business laid before John Woolford was so slight and so easily dealt with as to puzzle the lawyer that it had been brought to him. When it was done, it was past midday and as a matter of course, he invited his client to share the family nuncheon.

'Just my wife, myself and Miss Marney whom I'm sure you will remember,' Woolford said with genuine innocence, as he led the way into the dining-room.

Fanny and Elaine, already seated at the table, looked round. Elaine had known Lord Meldreth was coming but knowing it to be a business visit, had not expected to see him. Before she could react in any way, the unintended irony of John's words made its impact. No, she thought bleakly, his other persona, Cato Raffen, was unlikely to have forgotten her, though she could hazard no guess as to which of the many trespasses he held against her he best remembered. She hoped her face was as impassive as his as they exchanged bows.

If Fanny and John expected their guests to show more than polite interest in each other, they were disappointed. Though seated side by side and decently civil to each other, they exchanged very few words. What liveliness there was at the table depended chiefly on Fanny.

Elaine had herself well in hand and the one or two glimpses she caught of Cato's profile revealed nothing of his thoughts. The meal was not prolonged since no one showed a desire to linger over it. As soon as they left the dining-room, Elaine made a hasty excuse and slipped away into a side passage and out into the garden.

The day was coldly colourless and still. It matched her feelings.

She was relieved to find that she could meet his recently elevated lordship with composure, that she felt no stir or flicker of past agitation. She walked doggedly along the most secluded of the paths. The cold was penetrating and she hugged close the woollen shawl she had taken from a hook near the garden door.

Night-time frost still lingered in the shadowed places and the last buds of the roses hung brown and sad on the bushes, void of any hope of opening. A sizeable pond divided the garden from the parkland and what pale light the day yielded, the motionless water had gathered to itself so that it lay a shining steel mirror reflecting the bleached sky.

Taking refuge in the little Palladian pavilion that overlooked the water, she sat down on the cushioned benching to wait out Cato Raffen's departure. It could not be long delayed, she thought, if he hoped to make a return journey before the early darkness of a winter's day closed on the land.

The pavilion proved a chilly retreat. Lit by four tall windows on each of its two longer sides it admitted as much cold as light, a cold that also struck upward from the stone-flagged floor through the thin soles of her house shoes. She prayed Lord Meldreth would leave soon before she was utterly benumbed, but had no way of knowing what he did without returning to the house.

Having come, Cato was determined to carry through his intention. When he asked for a few minutes private speech with Miss Marney however, she could not be found in the house. Further enquiry had at last produced a kitchen maid who had glimpsed her going down the garden by way of the path past the orchard. At that point, with better understanding of Elaine's behaviour than the Woolfords could have, Cato had taken over the quest.

He found her without too much difficulty and saw her through one of the windows of the pavilion while she was still unaware of his presence. She was staring out at the gleaming water, her expression quietly pensive. He would rather have seen some evidence that she had been disturbed by his coming to Bellehaugh, seen some sign that he had once meant something to her. Was not forgotten. He moved on to the door, opened it, entered. She looked up with a slight frown of displeasure for the interruption.

The speech he had prepared to lead up to his main objective vanished from his mind. Baldly he announced, 'I have something to say to you.'

She inclined her head in acknowledgement but did not speak.

Before her indifference, he lost more way, could not think how to proceed.

To end the impasse, Elaine prompted coolly, 'If it has anything to do with when we last met, I am quite prepared to hear the worst.'

'No,' he said shortly, not wanting to remember how far wrong he had been at that time. 'That business is all at an end. Forgotten.' What was not at an end and could never be forgotten, was what had happened at the Lawrenses' ball. She acknowledged the lofty insufficiency of what he had said with nothing more than a small Mona Lisa smile that told him nothing. What had happened to the fiery-spirited opposition with which she had once faced him? Anger, bitterness, suspicion, he had come prepared for – but not a cool lack of interest. He said determinedly, 'It is something quite else about which I want to speak to you.'

He felt the wrongness of the mood and frowned over it but blunted his unease by telling himself she might be more ready than she appeared to consider an offer she had lost the right to hope for. One that might be more profitable to her than the bargain she had made with Braxted, for there was little evidence that he had loaded her with the customary rewards presented to the valued mistress of a high-ranking nobleman. True, the handsome, diamond-set locket round her neck was more costly than anything of the kind he had seen her wear before, but she wore no other jewellery. Nor had she been given a house and a carriage and pair of her own, the basic acknowledgement of favours received by a wealthy man. All in all, she appeared to have gained little by her compact. If he had not known how frequently Braxted was in her company, he might have believed nothing had come of it.

Thrown out of his stride, he forgot the calm and simple terms in which he had intended to lay his proposal before her and said gracelessly, 'My real purpose in coming here today was to ask you to marry me.'

She stared at him in unbelieving silence. She had thought of several reasons why he had sought her out, but none had come near this. He could not be serious. It had to be another instance of his misplaced humour. Not giving herself time for further thought, she rose to her feet. said with cool dignity, 'I will suppose you drank too much wine at table . . . are a little drunk.'

'That is an undeserved insult.'

'Am I supposed to believe that you have come to admire me in the three months since we last met? Or should I say come to admire me again?'

'Your person I have always admired. I cannot say I admire the path you have chosen. Or even understand your reason for choosing it. I should like you to believe I still—' The word 'love' stuck in his throat and he substituted, 'I still have a strong regard for you.'

'If you believe that, Lord Meldreth, I am astonished. I certainly cannot. Indeed, I should have been unsurprised had you told me you hate me. As to the path I have chosen— I wish I understood what you are talking about.'

Perhaps it was as well to bring into the open the thing he found so hard to forgive in her. Better to speak out now and be done with it. He said, 'I am talking about the Marquis of Braxted. I know you are his mistress. It was my intention to propose to you on the night of the Lawrenses' ball. I cannot believe you did not know it. Looking for you, it was my misfortune to open a door into a particular room at the moment Braxted confirmed his right to be your protector. You were both too engrossed in each other to be aware of my being there.'

He saw with perverse satisfaction that though apparently unchastened, she was silenced. But he mistook the reason.

Elaine had a large adjustment to make. With an effort she recalled the details of the most crucial moments of revelation between herself and the marquis. Anyone walking in when Braxted had said, *You are under my protection now*, might be forgiven for putting the common interpretation on the words. Yes, she had known Cato had intended to propose that evening – as surely as he must have known she would accept. She could understand the shock to his feelings when he opened a door on to a scene that seemingly could have only one interpretation. In the light of that, his present offer might be thought generous.

But she felt no temptation to leave the tranquil shore she had reached and accept his offer. Far from it. With only a condescending 'strong regard' on his side and a numb fortitude on hers, what a travesty of the dream she had once cherished their life together would be.

Before she had shaped a reply, her mind leapt back to the word *generous* and her gaze sharpened shrewdly on the man facing her. Recapturing some of the words he had used and their general character, it seemed to her that Cato Raffen, or Lord Meldreth as he now was, had not come without some sense of his generosity. Nor without some expectation of her willingness to grasp at it.

A glitter in her green eyes, but her tone airily light, she said, 'So. . . . If I understand you correctly, my lord, you are offering

234

me marriage because you admire my person and in spite of your knowing that I am the Marquis of Braxted's mistress? Quite naturally you will expect me to show gratitude for such chivalry.' She paused just long enough to put an edge to her mockery. 'As so often before, I fear I must disappoint you. A feeling of gratitude entirely escapes me.'

She gave him scant time to digest that before sweeping on to say, 'My lord, I am aware of the difficulty you have in either listening to, or believing what I tell you. Yet, unavailing though it is, I tell you I am *not* the Marquis of Braxted's mistress. Nor has he ever invited me to be so.'

What use did such assertions serve against the the evidence of his own eyes and ears? He had not imagined Braxted's words; nor had he fancied the increase in man's visits to whichever house she happened to be living in. The lies diminished her further and he turned to the door. 'It is pointless to continue.'

'You are right,' she agreed coolly.

His hand was on the door-handle when she threw a question after him. 'Will you satisfy my curiosity on one point before you go – why did you not inform the marquis of my part in the Dacier affair?'

Out of a welter of angry feelings, he flung back savagely, 'Because I loved you, damn you!'

'And for Gertie's sake, of course?'

'Gertie?' He sounded as though he had never heard the name before. 'No, not for her sake. It would have been a better reason, no doubt!'

'And a more honest one! The love you say you had for me was a feeble thing . . . had brief life. You could not – *would* not – believe I was at that wretched tavern against my will. Nor that what both Dacier and I told you was the truth. And if I told you now that you were mistaken in your understanding of what you overheard at the ball, you would not believe me, would you?'

He laughed harshly. 'No. How could I? I heard clearly what was said. Saw your willing acceptance.'

'A man extends his protection to others than his mistress.'

Almost he swept that aside, then decided she should not claim again that he could not listen. 'What are you saying?' he demanded.

She held his gaze, deliberately allowed the silence to lengthen between them, said at last, coldly and flatly, 'That I am the Marquis of Braxted's natural daughter. He revealed it to me at the Lawrenses' ball having just returned from establishing the fact beyond any uncertainty. *That* was what you looked in on, whether you choose to believe it or not. Coming late to father-hood, my noble father is finding some entertainment in exercising his fatherly right to be in my company, direct where I go, what I do. And . . .' – still holding his gaze, she ended with unkind amusement – 'no doubt, whom I marry.'

If she wanted revenge, she had it. The shock was considerable. Self-condemned, he saw himself from the time of that ill-fated ball, as hasty, bigoted, wrong, and continuing so through to the present hour. Whatever unhappiness he had suffered in the process had been self-inflicted. Looking at his 'generous' proposal through her eyes he saw it for what it was worth. Impossible now to lay claim to loving her; to having loved her without intermission though believing her guilty of all the sins with which his imagination had loaded her.

'I can say nothing you can want to hear.' He turned again to the door.

'Wait!'

He turned back. If she chose to flay him with her opinion of him and his offences, he owed it to her to listen.

But having spoken on impulse, Elaine had no idea what she wanted to say . . . only knew with the utmost certainty that she could not let him go. Feelings she had believed dead and deeply entombed, were escaping into new life. The look on his face when he had turned away had struck her like a physical blow. She had known the deepest misery herself; it was he who had made her familiar with it. If it was his turn now, you could say it served him right, yet her instinct was to draw close and offer comfort. But not without self-interest. This was the man who, for a few short weeks, had shown her a tenderness she would give the world to find again and against all the urging of reason, there was a growing certainty in her that he alone could bring her to a fullness of happiness unreachable with any other.

Now under the absolute necessity of saying more, she had no idea how to proceed and fell a little desperately into awkward banter. 'You made me an offer of marriage, sir, should you not stay for my answer?'

His tense expression tightened still more, but she was in too much confusion to notice. She held to her light tone because it seemed to leave a way out if she was making a mistake.

'You claimed to have a strong regard for me. Is its continuance to be relied on, would you say?'

Uncertain where she was leading, he said only, 'Yes.'

'Without interruption?'

For a moment he hesitated, unbelieving. Then, taking a step away from the door, he said in a tone of exasperation, 'Ever since I first saw you, you have confused, provoked and maddened me!'

Her heart, for its own reasons, lifted. 'I sympathize, for it is what you have done to me. It would be most unwise for us to marry, I think.'

Words and tone did not match. He put his faith in the buoyancy of the latter and moved closer still.

'Then what am I to do, because no other woman will suit. For some reason I cannot help loving you, damnit!'

'Put so charmingly, I am forced to believe you.'

They stood gazing at each other then in a silence made

eloquent by what each saw in the other's eyes. Tensions dissolved, grievances lost importance and much as there was to be said, now was not the time. Who first moved to close the remaining distance between them neither knew, but in moments Cato had gathered her into his arms and was kissing her. He began tentatively, with the gentleness of a lingering doubt that she was here in his arms, but her reality and her willingness put a swift end to doubt and freed him to kiss her with all the passion of relief and triumph.

Emerging some time later in considerable disarray, her shawl on the floor but feeling far from chilly, Elaine said a little breathlessly, 'Do you not wish to know if your affections are returned?'

'If they are not, you have just shown yourself to be a most unprincipled woman.'

'*Another* judgement, my lord?'

'With a life-sentence to follow that your judge is compelled to share.'

Reason told her the sharing would not always be easy, but reasons that had nothing to do with the understanding, put forward stronger argument for the happiness she would know in the time between.

She leaned into his arms again and lifted her face to exchange a last, slow, honeyed kiss before she said with glinting mischief, 'You realize you will have to ask my noble father for my hand. . . .'